STRICTLY PROFESSIONAL

CHRISTINA C JONES

Strictly Professional

Christina Jones
Copyright 2014 by Christina Jones

❀ Created with Vellum

UNTITLED

A note from the Author:
If you're reading this, thank you! From the bottom of my heart, thank you! I put my time, passion, and love into every word within these pages, and it is absolutely incredible to be able to share.

I also want to give a quick thank you to my wonderful beta readers, who offered a kick-ass turnaround time for me because they knew how ready I was to share this with the world.

Gabi and Terrence are very, very dear to me. I hope you enjoy their story!

GABI

I shouldn't have let Regina talk me into this. I don't wanna be here.

And yet, here I was. I hadn't unpacked my bags, and I barely had time to shower away the memory of my awful flight before my new roommate dragged me out the door, insisting that I needed to have a little fun.

But I definitely wasn't having fun. This was decidedly *not* fun.

I'm sure Regina had good intentions when she invited me out. If my new roommate was fresh off of a breakup with her boyfriend of eight years, I would want to show her a good time too. What I *wouldn't* do is invite along my boyfriend, essentially forcing her to watch their lovey-dovey antics.

I just wanna crawl in the bed and sleep until it's time to start my job.

Excusing myself from the table, I made my way into the nearly empty bathroom and then pulled the phone from my purse. My eyes narrowed as I read the screen. Michael. I shook away the tension that crept up the back of my shoulders at the thought of him.

Forget about him. Isn't that what this entire move was about? A new start?

"Please stop contacting me."- I sent, even though I knew the message would be ignored.

I forced a smile in the mirror, pulled my thick mass of black curls to one side, and stood up straighter. I wasn't an uncertain, insecure little girl anymore. I left that behind in Chicago. At 25, I was a grown woman, starting a new life.

But you didn't hesitate to deposit that check your daddy wrote to cover your expenses for a year.

My posture deflated. I couldn't very well be 'Miss Independent' with my father footing the bill. I made a mental note to start a separate account as soon as I got my first check, then washed my hands and headed to the bar.

I needed a break. Just a few minutes away from Regina and Kevin. Any other time I would have found their overt affection for each other sweet. Tonight, it was just plain depressing. Mercifully, the bar was quieter than the main dining area. The live band sounded good, but the heavy thump of the drums had been intensifying my stress-induced headache since I walked in.

I requested an ice water from the bartender, even though I wanted something stronger. I quickly drained it and asked for another, slipping him a ten dollar bill so that he wouldn't feel like I was wasting his time.

"I hope that's water."

Even in the warmth of the lounge, the stranger's deep voice made goose bumps rush to the surface of my skin. My body tensed as he slid into the empty barstool beside me and I looked up, wondering if his face could possibly be any match for his voice.

Oh my, He is gorgeous. Michael who?

I had a strong urge to shove my fingers into the lush facial hair sprinkled along the bottom of his face, camouflaging a strong jaw line, high cheekbones, and smooth copper-brown skin. I nearly laughed at myself. I wasn't *that* girl.

"I'm sorry; I'm not sure what you mean." I hoped I didn't sound as clueless as I felt, but this wasn't my scene. I didn't go out and get talked to by strangers at bars. I studied, and passed the bar. Totally different things.

"You're drinking it like you just walked here from the desert. If it's anything other than water, you're gonna feel awful in the morning." That smile of his was making me feel light-headed. I didn't feel like I was breathing properly again until I was smiling back.

"Uh, yeah. It's just water."

We just sat there, with silly grins on our faces until he finally broke the silence.

"I'm gonna be honest, and just tell you... I have no idea what to say next. I saw you, and I thought you were beautiful, so I had to talk to you. I'm Terrence." He extended a hand, which I accepted, biting down on my bottom lip to stop the gasp that sprang to my throat at the warm feeling of his skin against mine.

Unlike many of the men in the room, Terrence was actually well-dressed. Casually sexy, in a gorgeous khaki colored blazer and a dress shirt so blue it was almost black. His athletic build was apparent, even with the jacket on.

"I'm Gabrielle," I replied, pulling my hand away to push a few stray curls behind my ear. "Friends just call me Gabi though."

"Ok then, friend-Gabi. Come up to the roof with me?" He had leaned forward, placing his left arm around the back of my chair as he spoke the words into my ear. The band was between sets, and far enough away that I would have heard him fine from where he was. He had moved closer just for the sake of being closer, and several places on my body thumped in response.

I took a big gulp of my now melted ice water.

I raised an eyebrow. "Um, you're cute and all Terrence, but I *just* met you. I'm not going anywhere with you."

"No, I'm not trying to get you to come home with me or anything. We wouldn't even be leaving; the roof here is open to guests. I just want to talk to you, really." He reached out, covering my hands with his. Touching me again. I normally hated being touched by strangers. Usually, I would have anticipated his touch, and pre-emptively moved away, but for some reason, I didn't mind it. It felt... comfortable.

He tilted his head to one side, his chestnut brown eyes reflecting the lights as he waited for my response. Conservative, professional new lawyer Gabrielle wanted to tell him 'no, I don't go places with men I just met'. But newly single, finally on her own Gabi was very interested.

"Let me tell my friend where I'll be."

"I'll wait for you here." He gave my hands a light squeeze, and then held them for support as I stood slowly on my heels. When I glanced back, he was watching me, a grin still plastered across his handsome face.

I spotted Regina by her massive honey-blonde afro, giggling in a corner booth with Kevin.

"I'm going up to the roof to talk to someone."

She looked up, surprised. "So you've been in Atlanta for a grand total of four hours, and you've already got yourself a man?"

"We're just gonna talk, Regina,"

"Mmm hmm. You're not about to have your daddy hunting me down cause you got chopped up by a stranger. Kevin and I will come too, just so you're not alone."

"I don't need a babysitter." My dad had charged Regina with 'looking out for me' and I didn't like that at all. Regina was only a few years older than me. Why did he think she could watch out for me better than I could watch out for myself?

"I'm not trying to babysit you. We won't even sit with you guys. We'll just be up there so he knows you're not alone, and doesn't try anything."

I guess she has a point.

"Well, we're going now, so if you're coming..."

"Right behind you," Regina smirked as she stood up, beckoning for her boyfriend to come with us.

———

"I'm STARTING to think I made a mistake, asking you to come up here with me." Terrence shook his head, giving me a side-long look.

I turned away, gazing out over the beautiful expanse of city lights against the darkened sky. "Whatever, you're out of your mind."

"Me? *I'm* out of my mind? You're the one who's actually trying to convince me that *Doug* is the best cartoon you ever watched."

"Because it *is*," I insisted. "You can't come to the table with *Hey Arnold* and think I can't top it."

I had no idea why I was tucked into a quiet table on a roof, discussing cartoons, but I was definitely enjoying myself. Not since my teenaged Black Planet days had I been able to sit up like this, talking and laughing with someone for hours. It felt good. Normal.

"This is the first time I've seen this view as an adult. It's still as amazing and big as it was as a child." I smiled at the memory of the summers I'd spent in Atlanta.

"So you're not a native? How long have you been here? Where you from, what do you do?"

"I'm from Chicago, and I've been here a few hours." I

purposely left out my profession. How would he react to me being a lawyer? Would he think I was stuck up? Boring?

"You didn't answer my other question."

"You have dimples," I said, hoping that the shift in conversation would allow the subject to rest.

"You've never seen dimples before, huh? You've got 'em too." Suddenly his hand was on me, cupping my face as he ran his thumb over the indentation in my right cheek. I flinched, surprised at the warm tingle that the simple touch had left against my skin. He brushed my hair away from my face, tucking it behind my ear and allowing his hand to linger at the nape of my neck, buried in my curls.

I tried my best to ignore the fluttering in my stomach, wetting my suddenly dry lips with my tongue.

"So it's getting late." Regina walked up, with her arm draped through Kevin's. "We're about to head out to Kevin's place. We can drop you off at home, Gabi."

"Yeah, we should probably call it a night." Terrence finally extracted his hand from my hair, and I turned to face Regina, trying to hide my flustered expression.

"Terrence will drive me home." I didn't even turn to him for an answer. I didn't even know what made me say it, but I knew that I wanted just a little more time with him. Regina gave me a skeptical look but didn't argue. She snapped a picture of his ID, and made him tell her what kind of car he drove before leaving him the warning that she would 'find and kill his ass' if anything happened to me.

Once we were inside his car, he handed me his wallet, asking me to put it in the glove box for him. When I opened it, I was greeted by dozens of pieces of candy.

"Oh, wow. *Chicago transplant, latest victim of the "Peppermint Killer."*

"Oh, you got jokes?" He laughed as he pulled the car out of the parking spot and made his way to the main road.

"Yes, actually. Why in the world do you have a glove compartment full of mints?"

"It's a bad habit. I'm obsessed with those things, and I keep them everywhere."

"That is int̄-er̄-est̄-ing." I bit my bottom lip so I wouldn't laugh.

"Aww, see just for that you can't have any." He turned to me as we pulled up to a red light.

I pretended to pout as I noisily unwrapped a mint, and then waved it in his face before I popped it into my mouth. I closed my eyes, letting out a playfully exaggerated moan. "You should have said that before I—"

I stopped. I had opened my eyes to find him staring at me, with an unreadable expression that left his lips slightly parted. We just stared at each other, for the second time that night, until we were broken out of our trance by an angry motorist leaning into their horn, urging us to stop holding up traffic. The rest of the drive was finished in silence.

"Give me your phone," I said when we reached the front door of my apartment. He cocked an eyebrow at me, but unlocked and handed it over. He grinned when he realized I was programming my number into it, and then dropped it in his pocket.

"I guess this is goodnight."

I gasped as he stepped forward, hooking his index fingers through the front belt loops of my jeans, pulling me close. I looked up, trying to meet his gaze as I rested my hands against his chest, savoring the feeling of hard muscles beneath my fingertips. I desperately wanted to look into his eyes, to know what he was thinking, but he was looking down at my lips.

The subtle hint of leather in his cologne surrounded me as he lowered his mouth to mine. My body responded immediately when our lips met, sending electricity across the surface of my skin as my eyes fluttered closed. I parted my lips willingly, and he accepted the invitation, easing his tongue into my mouth to share the sweet taste of soft mints.

I pressed myself even closer to him, feeling dizzy as I transferred my hands from his chest to his shoulders. He unhooked his fingers from my jeans, moving his hands up to grip my waist. I hadn't been kissed like this in...well, ever.

"Well at least he didn't chop you up." My eyes flew open at the sound of Regina's chipper voice over Terrence's shoulder. I pushed him away, embarrassed. "I'm sorry to interrupt, but you guys are right in front of the door, and I can't get in." She shrugged.

"Sorry," I stammered, quickly stepping to the side so that she could get by. When she closed the door behind her, I turned back to Terrence, shoving my hands into my back pockets. "That was..."

"Awkward?" He smiled as he finished the sentence for me. "It's ok, it happens like that sometimes."

He approached me again, kissing me softly on the cheek. "I will *definitely* be calling you, ok?"

"I'll look forward to it." I gave him one last smile before I went inside, closing and locking the door behind me. I was glad to hear the shower running in Regina's room. I didn't want to talk to her about Terrence. I just wanted to be alone so that I could replay the events of the night in my head, every delicious detail. Before tonight, I'd thought that it was just too soon to move on from Michael. Now, I realized that I just hadn't been meeting the right type of guy.

———

"THIS IS A JOKE, right? It has to be." I glared down at Michael, who was sitting in the window seat next to mine.

"No joke, baby. I came to escort you to Atlanta." He flashed me a

smile that just a year ago would have turned my legs into tapioca pudding. Now? It just felt like another lie.

I took a deep breath, and then finished shoving my bag into the overhead compartment. This little plan of his hinged on his confidence that I wouldn't make a scene. No matter how badly I wanted to curse him out, and leave the imprint of my hand across his smug face, I wouldn't. Not on this crowded plane.

"It's a two hour flight, Michael, I don't need an escort. But of course, you already know that." I sat, looking down the aisle for the flight attendant. A few of those little liquor bottles had suddenly become necessary.

"So you want me to leave?" He lowered those sexy emerald eyes down to my lips, thinking that I would do what I always did with him. Give in.

"If I say yes, are you gonna get your trifling ass off of this plane?"

That surprised him. I saw the familiar trace of anger cross over his face as he turned away, scratching at the sandy brown curls that covered his head.

"Why do you do stuff like that Gabi?" His voice was lower now. I had pissed him off.

"Because I don't like you, Michael. Why don't you understand that?"

"We've been together since we were teenagers. Why are you willing to throw that away?"

"Because you cheated! Are you delusional?" I lowered my voice to an angry whisper. "I have texts, emails, pictures, Michael. Dozens of different women over the eight years that you're trying to throw in my face. Don't you dare try to blame this on me."

"I told you, that's behind me now babe. I love you Gabi. I'm not worried about those other women." He reached over to grab my hand.

I snatched it away. "Don't touch me."

"I can't touch the woman I'm gonna marry?"

"You'll have to talk to her about that, but don't touch me."

He sighed, resting his hand on his knee. "I found a house."

"Good for you."

"It's for us."

I cut my eyes at him, then let out a snort of laughter. "You are delusional. You should get that checked out."

"We've gotta have a place to live once we get married, babe."

"I will never marry you, Michael. Ever. Get that through your head."

"I think you'll come around."

"Whatever." I put in my ear buds, and ignored him for the rest of the flight.

TERRENCE

"So... you wanna talk about that big ass smile you can't keep off your face, or nah?"

I looked up from the screen of my phone to see my best friend, Dorian standing over me. He was drenched in sweat from his run on the treadmill.

"You wanna get your musty ass out of my face, or nah?"

"Whatever man. Don't try to change the subject. You must be grinning about the honey I saw you leave the lounge with last night?"

"Why are you so curious?"

He looked at me as if I had asked a ridiculous question. "Because she was there with Regina."

"You'll have to refresh my memory, man. How do you know Regina?"

"She was in college with us, man."

I shook my head at him and shrugged. "I don't remember her man, sorry."

"Of course you don't, you always had your head in a book. Regina was the finest thing on campus though."

"And you didn't try to holler at her?"

"Oh I tried plenty." He smiled as he sat down beside me on the metal work bench in the gym. "But she walked in on me and her roommate, so she wasn't having it."

I looked down at the number on my screen again. "I see."

"Hey man, get your new friend to put in a good word for me with Regina."

"Sorry, D, no can do. It didn't work out last night, so it's on to the next one for me."

Dorian sucked his teeth, then shook his head at me. "You're not fooling anybody Terrence, I see you staring at that girl's number man. Why don't you go ahead and call her?"

I had intended for last night to end like *most* nights ended with women I met at clubs. We would sleep together. It was always just one night, and even then, I made sure to keep those encounters at a minimum, because I didn't want it to become a habit, nor did I want to end up like Dorian, with a reputation as a womanizer.

Then I spotted Gabi sitting at the bar. I'd never seen anybody look so bored while holding a drink in their hand. When I saw her tip her glass *all* the way back, I approached her, more out of curiosity than anything else. I wasn't *that* guy, that tried to take home the drunk girl.

When I spoke to her, she turned those cinnamon brown eyes on me and took my breath my away. After talking to her for hours, I discovered that this was a girl I could really kick it with. I thought back to the kiss we'd shared, remembering the feeling of her warm, soft skin beneath my hands as I held her close.

Snap out of it, man.

I had spent the last ten years of my life completely dedicated to my career. Four years of college, three years of grad school, then three years busting my ass for hands on experience. I avoided anything that even hinted at "seriousness" with women, because I was avoiding distractions. That's all my life seemed to be about these days, avoiding distractions.

I stood, and began placing the weight I had been using back on the rack. "You know I don't do the relationship thing, D."

"Have you ever tried?" Dorian was looking at me with his eyebrows pulled together.

"No. And I'm not about to start."

----*Gabi*----

JUST BE CALM, don't freak out, don't freak out!

I tried to follow my own advice as I stepped off the elevator into the offices of Pritchard & Graham Law Firm. At first, the only sound I heard was the rhythmic clicking of my heels against the polished marble floors. I went directly to the reception desk that lay in front of me, waiting quietly as the receptionist finished a phone call. She was an older black woman, maybe 50, with dark brown hair sprinkled with grey and pinned up and away from her face. The brushed steel nameplate on the desk identified her as Vanessa. Long, nimble fingers worked furiously at her keyboard as she took down notes from the call.

She gave me a slow once-over as she ended the call. "Can I help you, young lady?"

"Yes, I'm Gabrielle Jacobs. I'm supposed to start as a Junior Associate today," I made sure to phrase it as a statement, not a question. I kept my eyes upward and shoulders back. My dad had spent a lot of time coaching me on "not being a shrinking violet", so I was determined to implement those lessons.

"Ah, yes! Ms. Jacobs, from Chicago. Mr. Graham has been

expecting you. I'll show you to his office." She stood, show-casing a tall, curvy figure in a royal blue dress that shone like sapphire against her skin.

This lady probably has all the old men after her. Hell, probably some young ones too!

I followed her as she made her way through a frosted glass door into what appeared to be the central workings of the office. There were people everywhere, and the sounds of papers rustling, pens clicking, and people talking merged together into a dull roar that was much more soothing to my ears than the quiet of the reception area.

She led me to into an office filled with sleek, black leather furniture and a huge window that featured a prominent view of downtown Atlanta.

"Mr. Graham? Ms. Jacobs is here to see you," Vanessa said as Mr. Graham looked up from his desk.

"Thank you, Vanessa," he gave her a nod. She smiled at him, then me, before she turned on her heels and left, closing the door behind her. Mr. Graham stood up from his chair, coming around the desk to approach me. His bald head shone in the well-lit office, and his thick, but well-groomed goatee and mustache were a distinguished mix of salt and pepper gray. When he reached me, he pulled me into an embrace against his tall, wide body, lifting me off of my feet.

I shrieked loudly, squirming to get away as he began laughing. He placed me back on my feet, planting a kiss against my cheek before he let me go.

"Uncle Bobby!" I wrinkled my forehead at him. "You're gonna mess up my outfit!" I tried my best to smooth my clothes down, restoring them to their originally neat state.

"Come on, Gabi-girl, I haven't seen you since your under-grad graduation, I can't be excited?"

"Of course you can. I'm just nervous. I want to make a

really good impression on everybody, not have them thinking I don't know how to use an iron. And you can't call me that!"

He tried his best to look innocent, but he never could help the smile that played at the corners of his mouth. "Call you what?"

"Gabi-girl. I don't want anybody to know I'm your niece. I've gotta make my own name."

"Ok, ok, I'll stick to just Gabi. You all settled into your apartment? Roommate treating you ok?"

I winced as I thought of Regina catching Terrence and I in the middle of a kiss. I was still a little annoyed that he hadn't called me, even though he claimed he would. Typical guy. "Yes, everything is good."

"You sure? What was that look for?"

"Nothing that you need to worry about Uncle Bo-I mean, Mr. Graham."

"Mmmhmm." He crossed his arms over his chest. "You met any little knuckle-head boys yet?"

"When would I have had time for that?" I lied. "I'm not here to date, I'm here to work."

"Well, in that case, let me tell you about how things work around here. You're starting as a first-year associate, or Junior Associate. I'm assigning you to a Senior Associate, who you'll work with, and assist with cases. If you'll still here after three years, you'll become a Senior Associate, and after five, an Executive associate. Now, the associate I'm pairing you with is already a pretty damned good lawyer, and some day, with more experience, he is going to be *excellent*. This is the only favoritism I'm going to show you Gabi-girl, *use it wisely*," he said, lightly tapping me on the nose with his finger before he escorted me out of his office.

We turned a corner, and he led me down a quiet hall filled with offices. He stopped at one of the doors, giving a short knock before he entered.

"This is your Senior Associate," he said to me, motioning toward the front of the room. "Get used to him, because for the next year...well, you belong to him. You do what he says, even if that's getting coffee, making copies, arranging pens. Whatever he needs, that's your job. Gabrielle Jacobs, meet Terrence Whitaker. Terrence, this is Gabrielle."

Wait a minute, Terrence?

My uncle leaned to the side, speaking quietly into my ear. "Don't worry, he'll take good care of you, treat you with respect," he assured me before he straightened, turning his attention back to the man who was now standing in front of us. Sure enough, it was *that* Terrence, looking very sophisticated in his charcoal-gray dress shirt and a patterned tie. I detected confusion in his eyes, his brows dipped slightly as he extended his hand toward me in greeting.

He didn't even crack a smile as he shook my hand half-heartedly, quickly releasing it before he looked over to my uncle.

"I can already tell, you two are going to make a great team!" He clapped us both on the shoulders and then left the room, closing the door behind him.

----*Terrence*----

MAYBE THIS IS A SIGN.

Gabi had been on my mind since I met her Saturday night. On Sunday, I pulled out my phone at least a dozen times, just staring at her number before I inevitably put it away. I couldn't deny that we had a spark, but it had to end there. Never calling was easy. But what the hell was I supposed to do when she was right in front of me?

"So, you're a lawyer?" Gabi was the first to speak, after several moments of awkward silence. "I never would have guessed. You didn't look like a lawyer the other night."

"Yeah, neither did you," I replied, remembering the painted-on jeans and silky, cropped shirt she'd worn that night, with her big curly hair flowing free. It was a far cry from the conservative slacks, dress shirt, and bun she wore today.

She still looks damn good.

Maybe even better than before. She was looking up at me with those big brown eyes again, her full lips curled into a smile that I couldn't bring myself to return.

"Gabi...you know this means we can't see each other, right?" It was the perfect out. I swallowed hard as she dropped the grin from her face, pressing her lips into a straight line instead.

"Yeah, um...I guess it does," she gave a short nod, looking down at her feet for a moment. "I mean, we didn't even really get a chance to *start* anything, but this kinda feels a bit like a break up, right? Or is it just me?"

"No," I assured her. "It's not just you. I'm disappointed too, but I don't think it's a good idea to date a coworker."

She's a distraction. A sexy little caramel-skinned distraction.

"Well, um...if we're here to work, I guess we'd better work." She gave a small shimmy as if she were shaking off negative energy.

"Yeah, let's get to it."

I escorted her to my desk. I had always been content with my small office. It was, after all, somewhat of a luxury for a third year associate to have their *own* office at Pritchard and Graham. But the partners believed in me, and believed in my talent, which is why I had been assigned an associate. Usually, only fourth year associates would get this privilege.

I sat down across from her, explaining the case that we

would be working on. Opening my desk to retrieve a file, I noticed a bright blue folder that contrasted against the plain beige of the others. *Gabrielle Jacobs* was printed across the front, and I vaguely remembered Vanessa bringing it to me last week. I was so busy that I hadn't even looked at it, just shoved it in my desk and kept working.

I flipped it open, and my eyes widened as I scanned her resume. She had maintained a 4.0 GPA through high school, college, and grad school, all at the best schools in Chicago. Damn near perfect scores on her LSAT's and bar. She'd done pro-bono legal work for a women's shelter in Chicago while she waited to start her position at Pritchard and Graham, and her background check was flawless. Her file even included an excerpt from an article she'd written about Ellen Atkins, who was a prominent, well-known black attorney, and apparently Gabi's idol. The girl even had perfect credit. It was impressive.

I finished giving her a rundown of the case, and then put her to work on a corporate laptop, proofreading legal documents. It was tedious, and from the subtle eye roll she gave, I knew she wasn't too pleased with the task. But, we both knew this was the type of thing she'd be doing a lot of as a new lawyer, so she may as well get some practice in. Besides, her focus on the computer gave me a chance to stare.

The screen glowed, casting a bluish tint against her golden brown skin. She wrinkled her nose at it as she focused on her work. She pulled a tendril away from the holder she'd used to pull her hair back from her heart-shaped face, twirling it over and over in her fingers as she read the document on the screen. Suddenly, her dimples appeared, and I looked up, realizing that she was smiling because she had caught me staring at her.

"Not polite to stare, you know," she teased, winking at me before she looked back to her computer.

———

"Mr. Whitaker!" Robert Graham was standing in the doorway of his office. I pointed out the way to the break room for Gabi, then turned back to see what he needed.

"So, what do you think about Ms. Jacobs?" He got straight to the point, directing me to have a seat as we stepped into his office.

"Well, I haven't known her long enough to offer a professional opinion, sir." I kept my tone light, hoping it wouldn't betray what I was really thinking.

"But you've seen her file, no?"

"I have. It's quite impressive."

"Impressive is right." He sat down on the edge of his desk. "Ms. Jacobs is going to be a star. She reminds me of you were when you were fresh out of law school. As you know, this first year can make or break a new lawyer. I'm entrusting you with this young lady's future. Are you up to that task?"

Sounds... daunting.

I sat up a little straighter. "I'd like to think I am. I'll make sure she learns as much as she can."

"I'm counting on it, Mr. Whitaker." A small grin turned up the corners of his mouth as he stood to open the door, pausing with his hand on the knob.

"Was there something else, sir?"

"Ms. Jacobs is a very attractive young lady, no?"

Damnit.

I couldn't help the smile that crossed my face. "Well... I'd be lying if I disagreed."

"That's what I thought." He clapped me on the shoulder as he opened the door. "I understand that the close proximity you'll be sharing with Ms. Jacobs could lead to a complicated situation, but I just want to *strongly* urge you against that. If you want to make partner here, it's going to require a lot of focus, which you can't give if you're chasing behind your colleague."

"I understand, Mr. Graham."

"Good, I'll check in with you again next week. Enjoy your lunch."

With that, he closed the door behind me.

———

"*GAHHH-DAMN, WHO IS THAT?*" Josh whispered, sliding into the chair beside me. I knew he was referring to Gabi, who was talking quietly on her cell phone on the other side of the break room. I chose to ignore him, focusing instead on the sandwich in front of me.

He frowned down at my lunch. "What's with you and these cold ass subs you're always eating? Why didn't you just come for sushi with us?"

"Because I don't want to waste money on an expensive lunch every day."

"Come on man, you're a third year! You're making what, $70k at 28 years old? What the hell are you spending it on, other than that fancy ass apartment at Axis?"

"Josh, mind your business." I wondered how he knew how much I made or where I lived. I made it a point to keep these people out of my personal life... or lack thereof.

"Ok then, let's get back to tall and sexy over there." He pointed towards Gabi. "I know you know who she is."

"She's my new associate, but why do you care? You've got Dana." I reminded him of his girlfriend, hoping he would stop looking at Gabi like he was stripping her naked with his eyes.

"I didn't ask you about that," he said, still staring in Gabi's direction.

"Yeah, well, I'm telling you."

A broad smile crossed over his face as he gave me an affectionate slap on the back. "Ohhh, I get it. *You're* tryna cut down that tree, huh?"

I choked on an olive from my sandwich. "Josh, you know I don't date coworkers,"

"Would you *Look.At.That?!*" He tuned me out as Gabi stood, turning her back to us as she walked out of the room. "The amount of ass, it's just...*outstanding.*"

"What's outstanding?" Dana asked, flipping her hair as she joined our table.

She and Josh were the strangest "couple" I'd ever met. They claimed each other as boyfriend and girlfriend, yet Josh was constantly chasing women right here in the office. Not to mention, Dana was cold and calculating, a direct opposite of Josh's friendly demeanor. I couldn't understand why they even got along, let alone willingly spent time with each other.

I said my goodbyes and fled the table, leaving Josh alone to lie to Dana about what was so "outstanding".

———

I FOUND Gabi back in my office, engrossed in her work. I wanted to take the opportunity for another chance to openly stare, but I knew if she looked up and saw me, it would probably creep her out.

"Hey, Gabi?"

She turned, with a questioning glance in my direction. "I'm about to head to the courthouse, did you want to tag along? Or you could stay here and finish what you're wo-"

"Of *course* I want to go!" she quickly snapped the laptop closed, pushing her chair back so she could stand. "What are you doing?"

"It's not my case; it's one of Pritchard's. But, it's a big case for the firm, so I'm just going to observe."

"Observing is good, I wanna do that."

"Grab your stuff then, let's go. I'll send my schedule to your iPhone so you'll always have an idea of what we'll be doing."

She smiled as she pulled her bag onto her shoulder. "I don't have an iPhone, I'm an Android girl."

"Yeah, my personal phone is a Droid too, but you'll get an iPhone from the firm, if you want to keep everything separate."

"Oh, cool. Uh, aren't you gonna get your briefcase and stuff?" She looked down at my empty hands with a slight frown.

"Already in my car. I was gonna leave straight from lunch, but thought I should come and check on you."

"So you didn't wanna leave me out, huh?" she asked as she followed me through the door.

"You're kinda my responsibility for the next year. You're supposed to be learning, and if that doesn't happen, it's on me," I explained. We stepped onto the elevator, and I pressed the button that would lead us to the parking deck on the ground floor. I watched her out of the corner of my eye as we rode in silence. I had to suppress a grin as she subtly bobbed her head, silently singing along with whatever music she had on her mind.

"Where are you going?" I asked when we exited the elevator, stopping her as she headed in the opposite direction of where I was parked.

"I'm going to my car, so I can follow you to the courthouse." She raised an eyebrow in confusion.

"That's not a good idea," I told her, shaking my head. "Traffic and parking are gonna be a beast, it's easier if you just ride with me."

She agreed, and followed me to my car. I spent most of the drive to the courthouse answering her questions about the firm. I got the impression that she had already done as much research as she could, so I did my best to just give her my personal perspective.

"And what about Mr. Graham? What do you think of him?" she asked.

"Robert? He's cool," I said. "*Excellent* lawyer, but he's not stuffy at all. Very laid back, unless you mess up. That's not a side of him you wanna be on, but as long as you stay out of trouble, you shouldn't have a problem with him." I thought back to the conversation I'd had with him before lunch. Would I get on his bad side if I pursued Gabi?

Wait a minute... when did pursuing Gabi become an option?

We found a parking spot at the courthouse, and I led Gabi in, listening to her chatter about what she was expecting from the case. We made our way through the metal detectors, and were about to step on the elevator when I heard someone call my name.

"Mr. Whitaker!" I turned to see my frat brother, Neil walking up to me with his hand outstretched in greeting. Neil was an attorney as well, but he was six years older than me. Because we were part of the same Greek-letter organization, he served as mentor for me throughout college and grad school. "Who is this beautiful young lady?" He looked over at Gabi as I shook his hand.

"This is Gabi Jacobs, a colleague of mine from P&G. Gabi, this is Neil Coleman."

They exchanged greetings, and then he raised his eyebrows at me, glancing over at Gabi.

"Hey, I need to speak with Neil for a minute," I said, turning to Gabi. "You can go ahead to the courtroom; I'll join you in a minute."

"Sure, I'll see you inside." She turned to wait for the elevator as Neil pulled me over to the side of the foyer, speaking in a hushed tone.

"So..." he said. "How is Tarryn?"

I knew this was coming, as soon as I saw him. "She's as well as can be expected." Neil was my homeboy, and I hated to withhold information from him, but Tarryn had been clear about him not knowing anything.

"That's what she told you to say, huh?"

When I nodded, Neil shook his head, running a hand over the back of his neck.

"I don't understand why she won't just talk to me, man." He had a pained expression in his eyes.

"You know how Tarryn is. She does what she wants, and doesn't explain. Just gotta go with it," I replied. I felt bad for Neil, but I would always respect my sister's wishes.

"But that's your sister. She won't take your advice?"

I threw my head back and laughed. "Are we talking about the same girl?" Tarryn was five years older than me, and quite scary when she wanted to be. She'd broken up with Neil almost a year ago, without giving him a real explanation. I got the worst cursing of my life when I questioned her decision on that.

"I guess you have a point," Neil conceded. "Will you at least tell her I asked about her?"

"I always do man." I raised my hand to shake his, and then started moving toward the elevator.

"Nah, hold up young blood," he said, stopping me. "I saw the way you were grinning at your "colleague". What's the story there?"

"Nothing," I lied, not wanting him to pick up on the feelings that already had me confused. "She's a first year associate; the partners assigned her to me. That's all."

"Terrence...I know when you're lying man, I taught you how. You're not giving the real deal."

"I don't know what you're talking about."

Neil threw up his hands in defeat. "That's bull, but ok

man. I know you're trying to be all hyper-focused on your career right now, so just watch yourself man. Spending *all* of your time with a smart, beautiful woman…I don't like your odds." He chuckled, shaking his head.

"I can handle myself," I assured him.

----*Terrence*----

I DON'T KNOW *if I can handle myself.*

Gabi was behind me, leaning on my shoulder as I walked her through using the iPhone Vanessa gave her when we returned to the firm after court. I knew she was perfectly capable of figuring it out on her own, but she asked me to show her, with those dimples on full display and I had to oblige.

She even *smelled* sexy, a faint aroma of citrus, vanilla, and what I could only describe as clean. The scent, and her breasts against my back were making it very hard to remember my pledge to be strictly professional with her.

I wrapped up the demonstration, then held the device up to her.

"Thank you very much!" She patted me on the shoulder as she straightened up, walking to the other side of the desk. My eyes didn't leave her body until she was seated again, staring down at the unfamiliar screen. I turned my attention back to the brief I'd been working on, relieved to have her out of my immediate space. Maybe now I would actually be able to focus.

No. She was doing it again. Bobbing her head to nonexistent music while she worked. She must have felt my eyes on her because she looked up, lips slightly parted as she gave me a questioning glance.

"What?" she asked softly, a hint of a smile crossing her face.

"Huh? Oh, nothing," I replied. "Not really. You're moving a lot over there, it's a little distracting."

"Oh! Sorry." Her eyes grew wide. "It's subconscious, really. I just...I love music, and it's always in my head. I'll try to keep still though!"

Don't, it's cute.

"No, I wasn't saying that, I just noticed is all. I'm sure I'll get used to it."

She grinned at me as she turned back to her work. "Good, cause I kinda can't help it."

I looked away, slightly embarrassed that she'd caught me staring at her, *again*. I had to get this girl out of my head. She was absolutely off limits, and the only way I would ever be able to successfully work with her was if I let go of my crush.

Everybody liked getting a first year, since it was basically like having your own assistant, but I wasn't feeling lucky at all. This was *torture*.

GABI

"I'm Josh."

He showed up out of nowhere, grabbing my hand as he cornered me in a quiet hall, licking his lips like he was LL Cool J. It was a shame that his approach was *so* wrong, because his smooth, mahogany-brown skin, strong jaw, and neat, shoulder-length locs made him quite handsome. "You're Gabi, right?"

"Yeah." I gently pulled my hand away. "Can I help you with something?"

He stroked his goatee. "Well...I was actually trying to see if I could help *you* with anything." He gave me a wink.

Ugh, he's one of those guys.

I tried to hide my disgust with a smile, and turned to walk away. "Uh, I'm gonna say no."

"If that changes, you make sure you let me know!" he called after me as I stalked down the hall to the elevator. I was mentally drained after spending the day sitting across from someone I had to pretend not to be affected by.

When I arrived at home, Regina was already there, having what appeared to be a rather intense conversation on her cell phone as she paced the living room. She was petite, with bronze skin and a huge mass of naturally curly hair that was now a deep chocolate brown, instead of blonde. Wearing dark blue skinny-jeans, black platform heels, and an oversized gray cable-knit sweater, she looked liked she was on her way out the door, but the abrupt way she ended the call and hurled her phone across the room told a different story.

She sat down on the arm of the couch, scrubbing her hands over her face before she rested them beside her.

"You wanna talk about it?" I took a step forward, finally removing my jacket and hanging it beside the door. I had been so stunned by the sight of an angry Regina that I hadn't done anything since I walked in except stare.

For a moment, it looked as though she was going to say yes, but then she shook her head, clenching her jaw before she turned away from me.

"Well... I'm gonna go in my room. Just knock or something if you change your mind." I gave her what I hoped was a friendly smile, and then turned to walk away.

"Gabi, wait." She was still seated on the arm of the couch. "How was your first day?" She forced a smile to her face, and it occurred to me that she might need a distraction from whatever that phone call was about.

I perked up, and gave her a sly smirk. "You're gonna need to sit somewhere sturdier than that if you want to know how *my* day went."

She raised an eyebrow as she slid to a cushion.

"Was it that bad?"

"Not bad... just eventful." Regina listened with wide eyes as I recounted the events of the day.

She shook her head, giving me a comforting pat on the hand. "So your mystery boo is basically your babysitter for the next year."

"Essentially, yes. But I honestly got the feeling he hadn't

planned on calling or anything anyway. He seemed *really* uncomfortable, all day."

"How did you respond to that?"

"I just kept on being myself." I shrugged, leaning back into the plush cushions of the couch. "We have to work together for the next year; there's no point in being weird about it. I'll be honest, Terrence is sexy. But it's not like I'm some sex starved spinster who can't handle being around a man." I stopped, realizing it sounded like I was trying to convince myself more than Regina. It was a front.

It had hurt more than I wanted to admit for Terrence to look at me as if I were the last person he wanted to see. I tried to just be my usual warm, bubbly self, but he seemed so uncomfortable that I wondered if that was the right approach.

I'd noticed him staring several times, probably wondering why he'd gotten the misfortune of being paired with me. Thinking why, of *all* the law firms in Atlanta, in the country even, I'd ended up at his. After all, he was there first. *I* was the intruder.

I put my head in my hands, suddenly dizzy with embarrassment that I'd thought there was something between us. He hadn't even called the next night! How ridiculous could I be?

"You know, I thought Terrence looked familiar, but I couldn't figure out why. I just realized, we were in college together at Emory!"

I looked up, hating that I was so interested in what Regina could tell me about him.

"Let me guess, he was a 'big man on campus'?"

She waved her hand, brushing away the thought. "Girl, hardly. It's probably why I don't remember him. He always had his head in a book. I don't think I ever saw him at a single party or anything, but his roommate, Dorian? He was a different story."

"He must have been fine," I said, grinning at the way Regina's eyes lit up when she spoke his name.

"Fine isn't even the word girl. Think about Morris Chestnut."

"That's not hard at all."

"Now imagine he has a younger brother that looks twice as good."

I sat up, curling my mouth in disbelief. "Regina, stop lying!"

She made the sign of the cross over her chest, laughing at my reaction. "I swear, Gabi! Dorian was unreal, and he knew it too. I think I might be the only black girl on campus he *didn't* sleep with. Hell, the only girl period."

"Ugh, he was one of those?"

"Unfortunately. I hope he's not still out there like that. He ran off to University of Chicago to go to med school, and I haven't seen him since then."

"Hey, I went to University of Chicago!"

"You've probably heard stories about him then," Regina said with a smirk.

"Nah. I was too busy keeping my head in the books, and running behind my ex." I rolled my eyes at the thought of Michael.

We were both quiet for a moment, and I assumed that Regina was just as absorbed in her own thoughts as I was.

"Gabi?" I looked over at Regina, surprised to see tears in her eyes.

"Yeah?"

"When you broke up with Michael... how long did it take to get over it? Like, *really* get over it?"

"When it happens... I'll let you know."

PULL IT TOGETHER, Gabi.

I crossed my arms over my chest, willing my body not to react to the scene in front of me. Squeezing my legs together as tightly as I could, I watched as Terrence paced back and forth in front of the jury, passionately delivering his closing arguments. Three weeks had passed since we started working together, but this was the first time I'd seen him in action. I could only describe it as downright *sexy*.

His athletic body, draped in a beautifully tailored charcoal grey suit, moved around the courtroom with the powerful, commanding presence of a lion. I was hanging on to every word, and I could tell the jury was too. As corporate lawyers, it wasn't often that we got the chance to argue in front of a jury, and he was making the most of his time. It was mesmerizing to me.

I found myself leaning forward in my chair as he spoke. I'd heard this entire speech before, having watched him practice it in his office. Here in the serious atmosphere of the courtroom, with the court recorder's fingers tapping his keys, the black-robed judge looming over us from the bench, it was different. It was beautiful. He delivered the last line with a nod to the jury before he turned to our table, looking me right in the eyes as he strode back to the empty seat beside me. My entire body tensed, and I had to squeeze my already tightly crossed legs together *again* to suppress the throbbing between my thighs.

Focusing my attention on the uncovered window behind the jury, I reminded myself where I was, and what I was doing there. It, my first time sitting *at the table* as a small part of the defense team, and I was drooling over my coworker.

Snap out of it girl!

It seemed like an eternity before the judge finally released us to allow the jury time to deliberate on the case.

"So how did I do?" Terrence asked from beside me, close enough that I could smell the hint of mint on his breath from the little mints he had admitted to being addicted to. He even kept those things in a big bowl in his office.

He was just inches from my face, leaning forward so that he could speak without being overheard by the dozens of people walking around the courtroom.

"You were great," I said truthfully. "Were you really concerned?"

"Yeah, I was," he admitted. "I don't ever want to get so cocky that I'm not concerned. That's how you end up underestimating your opponent, and losing."

"No, I get it. You just seem so confident that I'm surprised to hear that uncertainty," I said as he stood, accepting the hand that he offered to help me to my feet.

"I work hard not to let it show. You're not gonna tell anybody, are you?" He didn't release my hand from his warm grip.

"Of course not!" I met his eyes, hoping he would see the sincerity there. "I would never betray your confidence." I was surprised that he would even open up to me about something like that. There certainly hadn't been any grand breakthrough where we decided to be friends. I was just happy that we had reached a place where our interactions were no longer awkward.

A tingling sensation in my fingers called my attention to the fact that he was *still* holding my hand. When I brought my gaze back up to his face, I could swear that I saw a flicker of regret in his eyes, but it was gone almost as soon as I noticed. He quickly released me from his grasp, then occupied his hands with his briefcase as we exited the courtroom.

Don't read into it Gabi. Stop being silly.

I tried to ignore the steady buzzing of my phone as we rode back to the office. I knew it was Michael, calling me over and over between the texts, which I was also ignoring. I wanted to turn it off, but I didn't, fearing I would miss something important. Terrence kept looking at me sideways, as if it was starting to be annoying.

Yeah, get in line.

Finally, I gave in, responding to what looked to be the first text.

"Hey." -Michael.

"...Hey."

"How's Atlanta going so far?" -Michael.

"Fine."

"That's good. You made any new friends yet?" - Michael.

Eye roll number one. He wants to know if I've met a guy.

"No."

"Stop playing Gabi. You're beautiful, I know *somebody* has tried." -Michael.

And if they have?

"It's not your business anyway. What do you want?"

"I want to talk to you."-Michael.

"We don't have anything to talk about."

"Not even this?" -Michael.

My mouth went dry as I looked at the picture on the screen. Him, holding up an engagement ring that looked to be even larger than the last one he offered.

"That's nice Michael. I'm sure it will make someone really happy."

"You're gonna pretend you don't know it's for you?" -Michael.

"I already told you I would never accept your proposal, Michael. You cheated on me, and it's not acceptable. Not for me."

"So after almost 8 years of dating, you're done?" - Michael.

"Exactly."

"Can you at least think about it?" -Michael.

"I already thought about it, Michael. I'm done."

"Don't you think we would be great together? A doctor and a lawyer, like Claire & Cliff." -Michael.

Is he serious?

"The Huxtables, Mike? Really? No."

"You could be passing up something great, Gabi. I love you, and I can't even imagine spending my life with anybody else." -Michael.

"Oh please. I'm not your type. You like them trashy and dumb, based on the ones you were screwing on campus."

"What are you talking about?" -Michael.

"Don't play with me. Do *not* try to deny it, you're gonna make me mad."

"Those were just flings. You know you're #1. I could give you a good life Gabi. You wouldn't even have to practice law if you didn't want to." -Michael.

So, I should throw away my career for you?

"No."

"You're pissing me off." -Michael.

"Join the club."

"I'll see you when you come home for Christmas." - Michael.

"No."

"We'll see." -Michael.

I raised an eyebrow.

"You know how I respond to threats, Michael. Don't you still have that scar?"

"It wasn't a threat. What kind of guy do you think I am?" -Michael.

"I *know* exactly what kind of guy you are. I'll pass."

"Whatever Gabi, you'll come around. I'll just talk to your dad about it next time I see him at the hospital." -Michael.

"I'm blocking your number."

I tossed the phone into my purse, a little embarrassed that I'd entertained Michael for that long. But whenever I tried to just ignore him, he seemed to consider that compliance. I hoped that pissing him off would encourage him to just leave me the hell alone.

"Hey, you ok?" There was a concern in Terrence's voice that somehow made it all seem even worse. I had zoned out after the exchange with Michael, forgetting that I was in his car.

"I'm fine." It was a lie, and I could tell from his raised eyebrow that he knew it.

"But you're crying."

I hadn't even felt the tears sliding down my face, but I hurriedly wiped them away. It wouldn't erase the fact that I had just created another reason for awkwardness, but at least I could hide the evidence.

When we finally pulled into the parking garage at the firm, I hesitated before opening my door.

"Terrence?"

"Yeah. We can pretend that didn't happen."

GABI

"I take it the roommate is treating you well?"

I glanced across the table at my mother as the waiter refilled her wine glass. My mouth watered at the thought of having a glass of my own, but I didn't want to hear her mouth about staining my teeth. So I sipped my water.

"Yes, mother. Regina has been wonderful."

She tossed her head, making her perfectly feathered bob swing around her chin. At 45, my mother could easily pass for my slightly older sister. She actually got a kick out of it whenever we were together, and I enjoyed wiping the smirk off of her face by announcing that she was my mom. "Mm."

I rolled my eyes at the tablecloth. My mother was barely containing her disapproval about the restaurant choice, the city of Atlanta, my choice to become a lawyer, and everything else, down to the fact that I *still* hadn't "combed my hair".

"Don't disrespect your mother, Gabrielle." Eagle-eyed dad had caught the eye roll, and was now glaring at me from the other side of the table. I put on my sweetest smile, using the knowledge that their flight would be leaving in just a few hours as my "happy thought".

"It's fine, Gabe. This is the type of behavior we should expect now that she's been living with her little Craigslist roommate for a whole month now." She smirked at me before she took another sip of her wine, letting the veiled insult sink in. Neither she nor my father would ever let me live down the fact that I'd found a roommate online, despite the fact that it was an upscale building, and Regina was a young ad executive with a flawless background check. Nope, it was just something else I'd done wrong.

"No, Lena, she needs to work on keeping this little attitude of hers in check. Michael has already mentioned it as a deterrent from marriage. You remember her ill treatment of him on the flight down here last month."

They were both looking at me now, waiting on me to respond. I clamped my mouth shut, not eager to broach the topic of Michael. Not tonight.

My mother placed the wine glass back on the table. "You don't have anything to say for yourself? Your father is telling you that you're about to run off a perfectly suitable match, and your response is to say nothing?"

"I don't think that my response will be what you want to hear, so I made the decision to remain quiet."

"Unacceptable!" My head swiveled in his direction at the sound of my father's fist on the table. "You *will* explain why you've been anything other than pleasant to the son of long-time friends of this family."

I swallowed the bubble of insecurity that built up at the base of my throat before I spoke. "I have been 'less than pleasant' towards Michael because he disgusts me. He is a liar, and a cheater, and he--" I stopped to take a deep breath, "he just isn't what I'm looking for in a husband. Have you ever considered asking *him* about his treatment of *me?* I'm sorry for ruining your dreams of having a son who's a doctor, like you, but I'll never marry Michael. Excuse me."

I was out of my seat and on my way to the bathroom before either of them could speak again. I glanced over my shoulder, and saw my mother dab her mouth with a napkin before pushing her chair back to follow me. Thinking quickly, I took a detour into the kitchen, hiding until she passed. When she was in the bathroom, I ducked out of the kitchen, not stopping until my feet had led me out of the restaurant, into the early spring air. I stepped into the restaurant next door and pulled out my phone, glad that I'd had the presence of mind to grab my clutch from the table as I fled.

I tried, unsuccessfully, to shake the tension from my shoulders as I called Regina. I was relieved when she answered on the third ring, and agreed to pick me up as soon as she was done with her late day of work. I texted her address, then decided that I would have that glass of wine after all.

I was barely aware of my surroundings as I took a seat at the bar, requesting a glass of white wine. Nearly everyone else seated had their eyes plastered on the huge flat screen TV mounted against the wall, watching whatever sporting event was on. I savored the sweet taste of the wine as I sipped, closing my eyes to allow my thoughts to drift away somewhere peaceful. Maybe I could become someone else. Anyone other than the supposedly grown woman who still threw temper tantrums to get away from her parents.

"Would this be considered déjà vu?"

I opened my eyes at the sound of Terrence's voice, not even a foot away. I nearly choked on my wine when I realized that the seat I had chosen was right beside him. The half-empty plate of food, and the jacket draped over the back of his chair said he had been there long before I sat down. I tried hard not to stare at the strong, solid arms that peeked out from his short sleeves, revealing a tattoo I didn't even know he had, of a breast cancer ribbon entwined with a cross.

When I finally dragged my eyes back up to his face, his amused grin made me flush with embarrassment.

I turned to get the bartender's attention, suddenly in desperate need of a refill. "I'm sorry, I didn't see you sitting there."

"Lot on your mind?"

"You could say that."

"Does it have anything to do with you being dressed like that at a sports bar on a Thursday night?"

I looked around, really noticing my surroundings for the first time. The fitted pantsuit and silk blouse I'd chosen for dinner with my parents was definitely overkill for the casual, masculine vibe. At that moment, my cell phone started ringing, and one look at the screen let me know that my parents had finally realized I wasn't returning to the table.

"Well, this wasn't exactly how I planned to spend my night." I took a sip of the fresh wine the bartender placed in front of me, and contemplated ordering something stronger. I would probably need it to get through the inevitable conversation with my parents before they boarded their plane back to Chicago.

He cocked an eyebrow at me as he leaned back, then took a drink from his own glass.

"You wanna talk about it?"

"Terrence, you don't have to talk to me. I'm not about to start crying or anything, don't let me interrupt your night."

"You're not interrupting anything. My homeboy is in a whole other world, he doesn't even know I exist right now." He nodded towards a guy who was on his feet, yelling at the TV, complaining about a call by the referee. "I'm just here for the wings. Talk."

"I... uh." The phone rang again. "My parents. They treat me like a clueless little girl, and for some reason, whenever I get around them, I act the part."

"They're just loo--"

"No." I interrupted with a shake of my head. I didn't want to hear the same explanation everyone gave me for my parents' overbearing behavior. "It's more than that, it's a control thing. They nearly disowned me when I decided to pursue law instead of following my father into medicine. They actually *forbid* me to move here, but I did it anyway. Then there's this *jerk* they keep trying to force on me. It's just... a lot."

"Wow. I guess that is a bit much."

"Just a bit," I said, smiling dryly as the phone rang again. "This is them now, probably trying to figure out where I went."

He chuckled as he wiped his fingers with a napkin. "Ah, I see. That explains the clothes, you walked out of dinner on them."

I shook my head, embarrassed at the way he'd put it, even though it was exactly what happened. "I just couldn't deal. I've been away from home for a whole month, and they didn't even ask about *me*. They just wanted to know if my roommate had turned into a serial killer yet, and why I hadn't been groveling for my ex-boyfriend."

The phone rang again, but this time it was Regina, telling me that she was outside. I turned back to Terrence, who was still watching me. "Sorry to lump all of that on you and run."

"No problem. I hope it helped to get it off of your chest."

"It did, actually. Thank you."

I pulled out my card to pay my tab, but Terrence waved me off, telling the bartender to add my drinks to his bill.

"You don't have to do that," I said, meeting his eyes.

"I want to." He placed his hand over mine, but I quickly pulled it away, under the guise of putting my wallet back into my purse.

"Thank you." I slipped down from the barstool, promptly

losing my balance on the skinny heels I'd chosen for the night. I was already preparing myself for the pain of hitting the floor when strong, familiar hands gripped my waist, remaining there until I was steady on my feet.

"You alright?" I couldn't read his expression, but in my mind, he thought I'd fallen on purpose, just an excuse to get him to touch me.

"Yes, thank you." I brushed his hands away as I maneuvered away from the bar. "I guess wine and sky high heels don't mix."

"I wouldn't know."

"Yeah, I guess not." I pulled my top lip between my teeth, unsure of what to say next, but then my phone was ringing. Probably my parents again.

He gave me one last smile before he turned back to the bar "I'll see you tomorrow Gabi."

I couldn't get out of there fast enough.

----*Terrence*----

I TURNED BACK to watch Gabi's hips sway back and forth as she hurried out of the bar.

"Are you still gonna deny that you're feeling her?" Even though Dorian was talking to me, I didn't take my eyes away until she was out of sight.

"Don't start with this, D."

"Don't start what? Pointing out the obvious?" The game was over, and he had finally taken his seat.

"What exactly do you think is obvious?" I accepted a bottle of Corona from the bartender, then leaned back into my chair.

"That you like her, duh. When have you *ever* voluntarily listened to a woman bitch about her problems? I'll tell you, never."

"How do you even know what we were talking about? You were watching the game!"

Dorian took a swig from his beer. "You *thought* I was watching the game. I was actually trying to see the exact moment you turned in your player card like me."

"Whatever man, I never had a player card. Besides, I listen to Tarryn."

"That's your sister."

"Whatever, man. It doesn't mean anything. She's my coworker, I was just being nice." That was a lie. Truthfully, it had caused an unfamiliar pang in my chest to see the hurt in her eyes when she talked about her parents. I had been prepared to give her the standard 'just be grateful you have them' speech but once she explained her beef with them, I understood her frustration. They sounded crazy.

"So you wouldn't mind if I stopped by the office one day, took her to lunch?"

"Only if you wouldn't mind getting your ass kicked."

"*Whoa!* But you say she's just a friend, ok, Terrence."

I took a long swig of the beer in an effort to tamp down my irritation. My reaction to the thought of him taking Gabi *anywhere* surprised me. Dorian was my homeboy, damn near like a brother to me, but he had a reputation as a womanizer. I knew that he was trying to put those days behind him, but I didn't want him testing his resilience on Gabi.

"I don't know what's gotten into me, man."

"I do." Dorian leaned back in his seat, gesturing at me with his bottle. "You, my friend, have a crush."

———

I SAT in my car for a long time, staring at the front door of the house where I grew up. My case load kept me away longer than planned. I usually checked in once a week, but it had been at least three since I'd had a free weekend to see my family. Part of me really didn't want to go inside, but I knew they would be happy to see me. They always were. With a heavy sigh, I unclipped my seatbelt and exited the car, grabbing the bouquet of yellow roses I'd purchased on the way.

Tarryn was in the living room, sleeping in what used to be our mom's place on the couch. I placed the roses down on the coffee table in front of her, knowing they would be the first thing she saw when she opened her eyes. Smiling at the thought, I walked through the house in search of my Aunt Raelyn, who lived here with Tarryn. I finally spotted her in the sunroom at the back of the house, with her slim tabby perched on her shoulder as she crocheted.

I quietly opened the door, keeping my footsteps soft as I approached her chair.

"Auntie Rae," I said, startling her as I bent to place a quick peck on her cheek.

"Lil boy, I done told you about sneaking up on me like that!"

"Sorry, you're such an easy target I can't help it. You doing alright today?"

Aunt Rae leaned down to retrieve a new bundle of yarn. "Yeah, I'm good baby. Your sister though...I'm worried about that girl."

My heart dropped. This was one of the reasons why I hadn't wanted to come in. I had enough stress going on with work, the last thing I wanted was bad news about my sister.

"It's back?" I posed the question quietly, as if saying it too firmly would make it true.

"What? Oh, no, not that." She waved the words away. "I'm concerned about her emotional state. She's a young, beautiful, *healthy* girl. In a few months she'll be able to go back to work. I don't understand why she seems so down. This is a happy time!"

"I don't think it's that easy Auntie." I sat down in the empty chair beside her. "You know this makes ten years since mama passed, and that was Tarryn's best friend. That, plus dealing with her own stuff, it's just hard for her."

"I know. But everything has turned around so much, and she's getting such good reports from the doctors that I thought she would perk up some."

"Give her some time, everybody can't have a perpetually sunny disposition like you."

"You're right baby. And if I'd had to go through all of those crazy chemical treatments at her age, I don't think I would be very sunny."

Tarryn was 31 when she was diagnosed with the same aggressive breast cancer that had caused our mother's death. It was a shock to everyone, even though we knew that our mother's diagnosis meant that Tarryn's chances of developing it were greatly increased. Unlike our mother, Tarryn had chosen to get a mastectomy in addition to her chemo treatments, to decrease her chances of reoccurrence.

I changed the subject. After talking to my aunt for a while, I found Tarryn in the kitchen with a smile on her face, transferring the roses into our mother's favorite vase. Tarryn was beautiful, just like our mother. They could have been twins, with their warm, cinnamon-brown skin, slim figures, and trademark Whitaker dimples. Before the chemo, they'd shared the same head full of kinky black curls, but now, Tarryn wore her hair in a close-cropped fro.

"You look beautiful sis," I said, rounding the counter to give her a hug.

"Oh please."

"Really, Tarryn. You do." It wasn't just a "baby brother"

compliment. Now that she was out of chemo, her skin was beginning to glow again, and she was gaining weight. I was happy to see her looking healthy.

"Thank you. And thank you for the flowers, they're gorgeous."

"You're welcome, but actually, you should thank Neil. He asked me to get them for you, since you won't talk to him."

The smile dropped from Tarryn's face at the mention of her former boyfriend. She had broken up with Neil shortly after her diagnosis, without telling him about it, and forbidden me to tell him either.

She looked down at her hands. "Tell him I said thanks."

"Tarryn..."

"What, Terrence?" she snapped, rolling her eyes.

"You should talk to him. He still loves you." I didn't take my eyes off of her.

To my surprise, she didn't snap on me like she usually did. Instead, she sat down at the counter with a heavy sigh. "I wish he would just move on."

"He can't. He doesn't know why you broke up with him. You won't give him any closure."

"What am I supposed to tell him?"

"The truth, maybe?"

"I... I can't, Terrence."

"Why not?"

"Because he wouldn't understand. If I'd told him I had cancer, he would have wanted to take care of me. I don't want that life for him. Look what it did to daddy." Her voice cracked as she tried to hold back tears.

Our mother and father had been the best example of love I had ever seen. Always laughing, touching, and kissing. As a kid, it had been embarrassing, but I thought back on it with envy now. After our mother's cancer diagnosis, our father made it his personal mission to do everything he could to keep her comfortable and happy for the two years she fought. When she was gone, it was as if all of the light had been stolen from his eyes. Seven months after we buried our mom, we had to bury him too.

"Tarryn, you're cancer-free right now though. Neil deserves to make that decision for himself. You really should talk to him."

"I'll think about it," she conceded. "What about you, since you wanna be Dr. Love. Have you met anybody?"

I should have known this was coming.

This was the *other* reason I hadn't wanted to come in.

"You know I'm trying to focus on my career sis. I'm not worried about women right now." I swallowed, trying to wet my throat as my thoughts shifted to Gabi. She was starting become constantly present in my mind, and I hated it. It was distracting.

"Terrence, when are you gonna start thinking about your-self? I know you're trying to be noble, but I know that paying the bills at this house *and* your apartment, *plus* your student loans has to stretch you pretty thin. You should be building your own life." Tarryn placed a hand over mine.

"I wish people would stay out of my pockets, damn." I laughed. "The law firm covered the loans, and there's only a few months left on the mortgage. Then this house will be yours. You can do what you want with it, and I can put the mortgage money into my retirement account."

"You mean the house will be *ours*?"

"I mean yours, T. I don't need it."

"Terrence, when are you gonna stop trying to take care of me? *I'm* the older sibling."

I turned to her, grabbing her hands. "Do you remember, after mama and dad died, instead of going to grad school at Howard, like you *always* wanted to, you stayed at Spellman so you could look after me?"

"I do."

"You were in grad school, working your ass off at McDonald's every free moment you had, just to make sure I was good. You passed up all kinds of opportunities, and you sacrificed a *lot* for me, sis. I haven't forgotten about that. Making sure you're taken care of is my *top* priority. I know your health insurance is covering most of your medical stuff, but until you're all the way back on your feet, completely healthy, and able to get your career going again, you will never have to worry about your living expenses, ok?"

"Ok baby brother." Tarryn knew that arguing with me about it was useless. I would never back down from what I'd decided to do the moment she'd shared her diagnosis. "You know what I think?"

"I'm sure you're gonna tell me."

She cupped my chin with her hands. "I think that Dad, and *especially* Mom, would be extremely proud of the man you've become."

"I...I hope so." I swallowed heavily.

"Wait a minute...are you about to start crying?!"

"Hell no, Tarryn, stop playing," I replied, laughing. "I'll admit, you made me choke up a little, but that's all."

"Mmhmm," she teased, standing up from her seat at the counter. "You hungry?"

"You cooking?"

"Yeah."

"Then I'm hungry."

TERRENCE

"I thought you might be hungry." Gabi placed a styrofoam takeout container in front of me. "And I know you like Greek, so I brought you something from Nick's. You *have* to eat if you're gonna be up working all night like this."

She opened the box, and the aroma of the food hit me. My stomach rumbled loudly, protesting the fact that I'd been hunched over my desk all day, buried in work.

"I didn't even realize I was hungry." My mouth watered at the sight of the lamb gyro and Greek fries she'd brought. "You have no idea how much I appreciate this."

"Well, if I let you starve, they may send me to work under that Greenaway guy, who wears those weird, shiny neon shirts with his suits. And um, I think I'll pass on that." She laughed as she took off her jacket and sat down.

"Ohh, self preservation, I see," I said, wiping my mouth with a napkin. "Here I was thinking that you drove *all* the way to my favorite lunch spot, then all the way back *here* to feed me because you liked me."

Gabi blushed, then looked down, tracing the lines in her hands with her fingers. "Uh, I actually came back to help you, *hoping* that you would maybe call it a night a little earlier than you usually do." Her voice was edged with concern. I knew I had been working crazy hours, on very little sleep, but it had never occurred to me that she would notice, or care.

Once we got past the initial awkwardness of working with someone you'd kissed, she'd never given me any indication that she considered me anything other than another colleague. She treated me like she treated everyone else, with a pleasant, but distant professionalism that quite honestly drove me nuts. I was always aware of her, when she wore her hair differently, or tried a new perfume, but she wasn't even thinking about me. Until she walked in with takeout, concerned that I wasn't eating or getting enough rest. What did that mean?

You're over thinking it. She's just being nice, like she always has.

"You don't have to worry about me Gabi, and it doesn't look bad or anything if you're not here every moment that I am." A flash of hurt crossed her face, and I realized she thought I was implying that she was around too often. I quickly clarified my statement. "Not that I don't appreciate the extra time you put in, because I do. I wouldn't be nearly this far without your help."

"I know I don't have to, but I do. I've spent pretty much every day of the last 3 months working with you, and a *lot* of those were 10 and 12 hour days. You're exhausted, Terrence, it's all over your face. I know you want to 'be the best you can be' and all of that, but if you can't even remember to eat, and won't stop working long enough to get any sleep, how effective can you really be?" She spoke carefully, as if she were afraid I would be offended.

But she was right. I *did* need to get some rest.

"I'll tell you what," I broke the silence that hung between us. "I'll head home as soon as I'm finished going over these depositions."

"Fine," she quickly agreed with a sly smile. "I'll help! Besides, I owe you for that overpriced wine at the bar."

I shook my head, smiling as I placed my attention back on my food. That had probably been her plan the whole time.

----*Gabi*----

I HOPE *that wasn't too obvious.*

Even if it was, I didn't care. The dark circles under Terrence's eyes had been worrying me. He had been working through lunch, and staying at the office long after I left, even though I didn't leave until 7, sometimes 8pm. He was working himself sick, and it bothered me, a lot more than I cared to admit.

I had been careful to be nonchalant whenever I was around him. The last thing I needed was to become 'that' girl, with a silly obsession with her co worker. No. I would *not* become a source for office gossip, so I played it cool, and hoped he wouldn't notice how awkward I was. But I couldn't just sit back and watch, doing nothing, while he worked himself into a breakdown. So, if I needed to stay until 10pm, and force him to eat, that's what I would do.

I don't even know why I cared. Yeah, he was nice enough, but he hadn't given me any signals that he was interested in being anything other than a colleague. And even if he *did* want something other than that, he was my co worker. It was a disaster waiting to happen.

Then why is he staring at you?

I looked up from my screen, and sure enough, his eyes were on me. I blushed as I met his gaze, unsure if I was misreading the glow of desire I saw in his eyes.

"Did you need something, Terrence?"

He jolted when I spoke, looking away as if he hadn't even realized he was looking at me. "What? No. I-- I think we should call it a night. I don't want to keep you here too late."

I was shutting down my laptop before he even finished. Then I was on my feet, bag on my shoulder, gathering up the styrofoam plates from our meal. "I'll go put these in the trash in the break room, and meet you at the elevator."

I let out a heavy sigh when I closed the door of his office behind me, grateful for relief from the heavy tension. It was late, nearly 11pm, so the halls were empty as I made my way to the break room to dump the plates. When I turned to head back, I walked full force into a wall that hadn't been there a moment before. Terrence.

"Sorry. I wasn't expecting you to be there. I thought you were waiting at the elevator."

"Don't apologize, I snuck up on you. I just didn't want you to have to walk back by yourself." His hands were on me again, firmly gripping my arms as if he thought I was about to fall. Was he this handsy with everybody?

"Oh, ok. Thanks." I stepped away, and headed towards the elevator without looking back. We rode down in silence, but I could feel his eyes on me the entire time. I bounced from one foot to the other, waiting for the doors to open when we reached the parking garage. I was desperate for the safe confines of my car.

"Gabi." Terrence grabbed my hand as soon as the elevator closed behind us. "Thank you, for dinner. And, for making sure I get some rest. I... I appreciate it."

Why does this seem so intimate? Snap out of it Gabi, he's just saying thank you.

"It was nothing." I pulled back, but he didn't release me.

"Well, thanks for nothing."

Our eyes met, and for a moment we just stared, until we both bursted into laughter.

"Let me find out you've been watching romantic comedies," I said, wiping tears from my eyes with my free hand.

"I don't even know why I said that, but I'm gonna kill my sister for making me watch chick-flicks with her."

I blushed when he raised my hand to his mouth, leaving a soft kiss against my fingers. "Goodnight Gabi."

"Goodnight."

----*Terrence*----

"Hm."

Gabi circled something in the file in front of her with a bright purple pen. It was the third time she'd done that, and even though I was supposed to be working too, I was more curious about what she found. I was exhausted, and words were beginning to blend together, in a massive jumble of letters. I needed a break.

"You gonna share what you're 'hm'-ing about over there?"

"Well, I'm not *sure* I've found anything yet, and I don't want to say anything and be wrong..." She crossed her arms over her chest, then leaned back into her chair.

"But what if you don't say anything, and it turns out you were right?"

"I know, but I'd rather just look over it a little more first. It might not even be worth looking into, and I don't wanna waste your time."

"Gabi." I pushed my hands into my pockets as I stood up. "Why are you scared to tell me your idea?"

"Because I don't want to look stupid." She eyed me as I pulled up a chair beside her. "You've already established that you're good at what you do. I'm the new girl."

"I saw your resume Gabi. I can guarantee you that 'stupid'

is the last thing anyone thinks about you. Your grades, your LSAT scores, your bar score, they're all impressive. The only thing you lack is experience, which you'll never get if you're scared to speak up about your ideas. You can't be shy if you wanna be a lawyer."

"But-- "

"But nothing. We need to settle this case, so anything that could help the client, it's gotta get put on the table."

Gabi rolled her eyes, then began explaining to me what she'd found. As she spoke, it struck me just how passionate she was about her profession. It annoyed me, because it only intensified my feelings for her. She was smart, compassionate, beautiful, and single. Robert Graham had pushed her into my office, with what was essentially a warning to keep my hands off of her. Somehow, that made her more enticing.

Would it really be so bad to date a colleague?

Hell yes. If I had to quantify it, I would say that I could only give about 90% of my usual focus to my work. That other 10% was devoted to sneaking as many stares at Gabi as I could, and daydreaming about our imaginary relationship. I had it *bad,* after one interrupted kiss, nearly three months ago. How badly would my work suffer if we actually became an item?

You need to just kiss her again. Finish what you started and get it out of your system.

That was a crazy thought. Gabi was an attractive woman, anybody could see that. Underneath that, she had a subtle sexiness about her that she didn't even seem to notice. It just seemed to radiate around her, lingering in the air when she left the room. Kissing her again was the *very* last thing I needed to do. I *knew* it would be stupid, but as she talked, the memory of her soft lips grew in my head until it seemed like the best idea in the world.

It took me a second to realize that Gabi had stopped talking, and was staring at me, with her eyebrow raised in confusion.

"What are you doing?" she asked softly, not taking her eyes off of mine.

"I'm not doing anything..."

"You keep leaning forward in your seat, getting closer and closer to me. You're halfway out of your chair, Terrence. Do you not realize that your face is barely two inches from mine?"

I smiled. "You're exaggerating."

"No I'm not, you're still moving. Wha-" Her eyes widened in surprise, but she didn't resist as I pulled her forward, cupping her face in my hands to kiss her. As soon as our lips met, the fatigue I'd been feeling melted away, instantly replaced by adrenaline. Before I could think about it too hard, I had her halfway in my lap, slipping my tongue into her mouth. The pen she'd been holding clattered to the floor, and for the moment, work was completely forgotten.

A soft moan escaped her lips as I gripped her at the waist, pulling her close enough that her full breasts rested against my chest.

"You keep moaning like that and I'm go-"

We both froze at the sound of a heavy knock against the door. I had Gabi out of my lap and back in her chair, looking only slightly disheveled, as quickly as I could. She reached forward, wiping evidence of her lipstick away from my mouth just as Mr. Graham opened the door.

"You kids working hard?" He closed the door behind him as he stepped into the room.

"Yes sir." I was energetic, still wired from the kiss. "Gabi actually has a really good idea that I think will work really well for the client."

"Is that right?" Mr. Graham smiled over at Gabi. "Jacobs, you're already on top of things, huh?"

"That's right," I said, with a smile that made Gabi narrow her eyes in warning. "Miss Jacobs has definitely been an asset to me."

Truthfully, I had no idea what Gabi's idea had been, but I listened intently as she explained it to Mr. Graham. It *was* a good idea. When he finally left, Gabi and I both breathed a sigh of relief as the door closed behind him, and I turned the lock.

I watched as Gabi stood, hurriedly shoving documents into folders which she then stuffed into her briefcase.

"Hey, why are you in such a rush?" I asked, grabbing her hands.

She pulled away so she could put on her jacket. "I need to get home."

"Are you gonna ignore what just happened between us?"

"Yes, I am. It was completely unprofessional. It's not a good idea to get involved with a coworker, remember?" She threw my words from that first day at the office back in my face.

"Yeah," I responded soberly. "I remember."

But I don't like it.

"I mean, there's obviously something between us, Terrence, but we just have to leave that to the side so that we're able to work together."

I stopped her as she turned to walk away, stepping in front of her, blocking her escape. "You think it's just that easy?"

"No." She swallowed as she met my eyes. "I don't, but it's what we have to do. It was your idea, remember?"

"I...I guess it was," I admitted.

"Then...good night. Get some rest, please?"

"Good night Gabi." I didn't try to hide the regret in my voice. I stepped aside so that she could get to the door, then watched as she left, without looking back.

She had been right to remind me of the decision we'd made at the very beginning. It was important that we kept things strictly professional. But *damn* I wanted her bad.

----*Gabi*----

IT HAD BEEN two days since the second kiss. That's what I called in my mind, as if it were some disastrous, devastating event. 'The Second Kiss'. It was ridiculous really, that after finally settling into a casual almost-friendship, we were back to the awkwardness of our first few weeks. Terrence wouldn't joke with me, and avoided eye contact as much as he could. If we happened to touch, even just an accidental brushing of hands, he was practically falling over himself to apologize. The easy-going work relationship we had built seemed to evaporate overnight, and morphed into what felt like the uncomfortable bond of students forced to work together on a group project. All over a silly little mind-numbing kiss.

I flipped through the file he had given me, which contained details of what we would be doing next. After the last case, I was relieved to see that it was simple contract work. I was exhausted, and the tension between Terrence and I wasn't helping. I was almost glad that he was out of the office, in a conference with the partners and our last client.

"Ms. Jacobs?" I looked up to see Vanessa standing in the door, chic as always in a pencil skirt and printed silk blouse. "Mr. Pritchard and the other partners have requested that you join their meeting."

"Really?" Panic immediately set in as I jumped up from my chair. I had been running late that morning. My hair was pulled into a messy high ponytail, my slacks could have used better ironing, and the button-up I wore was a little tight around the middle from too many late night snacks.

"Come here." Before I could say a word, Vanessa had somehow tamed my hair into a neat bun and tucked my shirt in a way my buttons didn't look quite so uncomfortable. "There you go. Now, we need to get you in there. Come on."

I thanked her all the way up to the door of Mr. Pritchard's office, where she announced me, pushed me in, and then left me there, closing the door as she went. There were 10 pairs of eyes on me, including Terrence, who was looking at me with what I perceived to be a mixture of amusement and annoyance. I averted my gaze, focusing instead on the friendly face of my uncle, who appeared to be fighting a smile.

Several confusing minutes passed while I shook hands with people I had only seen in passing, or in pictures on walls of the firm. I stood there in shocked silence as I realized they were congratulating me. Opposing counsel had settled, and apparently, Terrence had given me full credit for the idea that I presented to him and my uncle a few days before. Someone, I didn't even register who, pushed a sealed envelope into my hand, and Terrence and I were excused.

As soon as we were back behind the closed door of his office, he pulled me into a hug. I stiffened, then pulled away without returning the embrace. What was he trying to do? The hurt that crossed his face made me immediately regret my actions.

He threw his hands up in defeat. "I wasn't gonna try anything, Gabi. It was a friendly hug, to say congratulations. I... I'm sorry."

"No, it's fine. I just--"

"You don't have to explain, I get it. We should get to work," he interrupted. He didn't meet my eyes again as he rounded the desk to sit down.

I looked down at the forgotten envelope in my hands,

then carefully broke the seal on it. There was a check inside, for $10,000.

I rushed over to hold the check up in front of Terrence. "What the hell is this?!"

He barely glanced up before answering.

"It's a gift from the client. A thank you."

"For *what?*"

"For doing a good job," He shrugged. "You saved them a lot of money. Millions. That check is nothing to them."

"But, it wasn't even my case. Terrence, this check is supposed to be *yours,* you did all the work!" I exclaimed.

"It was your idea that got the other side to settle, so you're the one who deserves the credit."

"But Ter—"

"Gabi, please. We've got another case to start on, can we just focus on that?" Agitation crept into his voice. "Oh, and... I won't touch you again."

Well damn.

That stung, but I didn't respond. I was confused. Was he actually angry with me?

That's not anger, Gabi. That's...hurt.

I had hurt his feelings.

GABI

"Terrence is gonna die." Regina carefully pulled a few curls down from the updo she'd just finished pulling my hair into.

"I didn't get dressed for him." I glanced at my completed look in the mirror. I wasn't entirely convinced that I wasn't giving off a "Ms. America" vibe in the fitted, floor-length black gown, but Regina had assured me it was appropriate for the event. I had to admit that it was flattering on me, enhancing the curves of my bust and hips, while camouflaging the fact that I'd put on a few pounds since the move.

Terrence will like it.

I shook the thought from my mind as I sat down on the edge of the bed to slip on my shoes.

Regina handed me the clutch she was loaning me for the night. "Oh please. You might fool those co-workers of yours, but you must have forgotten that you come home and tell *me* the real deal. You two like each other, I don't know why you don't stop playing around and pursue it further."

"I've explained this already, to him and now you! We're co-workers."

"You act as if co-workers don't date *all* the time."

I stuffed my cell phone, keys, and spare lip gloss into the clutch. "They do, but they shouldn't. What if it ends badly? How do I look at him every day after that? Maybe if I weren't stuck in an office with him most of the day it would be different."

"Gabi, that's only for a year though, and you're already four months into it."

"Even after that year is over, the fact will still remain that my uncle is our boss." I checked the time, noting that we only had a few more minutes before the car arrived to take us to the firm's 4th Annual Breast Cancer Benefit Gala.

"So?"

"So, screwing your boss's niece is pretty high up on the list of things that could prove detrimental to your future."

Regina cocked an eyebrow as she sat down at my vanity. "Do you really think your uncle would care?"

"I don't really know, but it's not a chance I'm comfortable taking with someone else's career."

I knew that my mother and father were pretty insistent that I would marry Michael, whether *I* wanted to or not. Uncle Bobby was significantly more laid back than either of them, and I knew he wasn't a big fan of Michael, but that didn't mean he would be ok with me sleeping with his protégé.

"OK, now *that* I can understand. But I still think you should talk to him about it. Maybe he doesn't even care about working at this particular firm, I'm sure someone else would have him."

"No." I remembered him telling me that Pritchard & Graham had been his number one choice of firms, and how happy he'd been when he got hired. I wouldn't dare present leaving the firm to him as an option. "I definitely don't want him to do that. He would probably laugh at the arrogance of me thinking I was so special that he should leave the job he had first, for me."

"Oh please, Gabi. From what you've told me, this mutual crush you two have going on is becoming pretty major. Uh, hello, he's kissed you *twice*." Regina wiggled two fingers at me for emphasis.

"Yeah, and now he acts like I have a contagious skin disease," I said, rolling my eyes at her.

"Whatever. I wouldn't be surprised at all if you ended up with kiss number three tonight. Maybe it will knock some sense into you."

————

WHEN WE ARRIVED at the gala, it was already in full swing, with a band playing, a huge crowd of well dressed people, and a beautiful venue. The partners had been pushing this fundraising gala, for patients and survivors of breast cancer, pretty heavily for the last few months, so I wasn't surprised to see plenty of familiar faces from the firm in the crowd.

One of the first things I did was accept a glass of wine from one of the waiters passing by. I didn't do well at large gatherings like these, and I could already feel the anxiety building. I spotted my uncle across the room, and dragged Regina along with me to greet him. We weaved through the throngs of people, finally reaching Uncle Bobby, who hadn't moved, but had been joined by another guest, who had his back turned to me.

Before I could open my mouth to speak, he turned around.

Terrence!

When his eyes landed on me, his eyebrows shot up as he dragged them down my body. There was no mistaking the darkening of his eyes as he took me in.

He definitely likes the dress.

"Gabi, you look...gorgeous." He finally broke the silence.

"Thank you. You clean up pretty well yourself, Mr. Whitaker," I responded, eyeing his beautifully tailored tux. I tried to remain nonchalant, looking away before my gaze turned into a stare.

Terrence shifted his attention to Regina. "I know there's at least one person floating around here who'll want a minute of your time before you go. He's actually the one the reminded me we attended Emory together."

"Dorian is here?" The way she asked the question, like she was out of breath, made me wonder if there was more to the story than what she'd told me about him.

"I'm sure he'll find you before the night is over."

"Terrence?" He turned as a beautiful woman walked up, snaking her arm through his. "I need to talk to you. It's kind of an emergency."

Who the hell is she?

A worried look crossed his face as he looked down at her. She was beautiful, to say the least. Her short cropped natural hair complimented her face well, and the magenta ball gown she wore contrasted perfectly against her warm brown skin. Terrence gave me a small nod to say goodbye before he led her across the ballroom floor and out of sight.

"I guess that's his date for the night," Regina whispered into my ear. "I guess she's cute."

"Don't do that, Regi. She was really pretty," I scolded, trying my best to tamp down the jealousy that had settled into my chest. I had no reason to be upset that Terrence had a date. I'd brought along Regina, because I didn't know anybody who wasn't already attending the event. Besides, he didn't owe me anything. I was the one who was insisting that we keep things professional. Why shouldn't he be free to date?

Annoyed, I excused myself from Regina, and looked for somewhere I could escape to clear my head.

Bingo.

I was relieved to see a relatively empty corner of the room, and I headed straight for it, pretending to be interested in the painting that hung there on the wall. I had only been there for a few minutes when I felt a warm hand against the bare skin of my back.

"You know the dress you're wearing has most of the men in this room sweating, right?" Terrence mumbled into my ear.

I looked up as he stepped forward to stand beside me. "Are you including yourself in that group?"

"No." He smiled as he shook his head. "I'll tell you later what group I'm in."

"Mm. Isn't your date wondering where you are?"

"No, uh, she's a little occupied right now." He turned so that he could point my attention to his date, who was currently wrapped in a *very* intimate embrace by a lawyer he'd introduced me to as Neil.

"Oh my! Terrence, that's awful. Why would she be-"

"Gabi," he interrupted. "That's my sister. Neil is her ex. But based on how they're holding each other, they may not be "exes" anymore." A broad smile crossed his face at the same time that relief crossed mine.

"Oh, well that's sweet," I said.

"Yeah, it is. I'm happy for them," he replied. "Dance with me?"

"Of course."

Terrence grabbed my hand, leading me out to the dance floor. I laughed as he dipped me back, and then pulled me into his arms, close enough that our bodies were touching.

"So." I was still smiling as we began to sway along with the rhythm of the song. "I'm guessing you're not mad at me anymore?"

"Mad?" He raised an eyebrow at me. "What made you think I was mad at you?"

"Well, ever since the um...incident, in your office, you've been a little standoffish toward me, but tonight you're being *very* friendly," I shuddered as his hand slipped down to the small of my back.

"I was just trying to respect your wishes Gabi, I didn't want to make you uncomfortable. But we're not at the office right now, so all bets are off."

"Is that right?" I tried to ignore the thumping between my legs. "Are you gonna tell me what group you're in now?"

"Group?"

"Earlier, you said my dress was making people sweat, but you weren't in that group. What group are you in?"

"Ohh," he said, leaning forward to speak into my ear. "*I'm* in the group that wants to take you home and take that dress off of you. But...strictly professional, right?" I closed my eyes as he placed a feather light kiss just below my ear and then stepped away, releasing his grip on my waist. "I hope you enjoy the rest of your night," he said with a wink, and then walked away.

Oh, damn.

TERRENCE

"That looked cozy." Dorian walked up beside me after I left Gabi in the middle of the dance floor, looking as if she wouldn't have objected to a lot more than the kiss I'd barely given her.

"Are you like, a professional lurker or something?"

"Whatever, man. So what happened? Are you two cool again?"

"We were never not cool. She thought I was mad at her though."

Dorian cocked an eyebrow. "But... you *were*."

"Don't you have somewhere else to be?"

"Nope. Still haven't danced with Regina. But back to you, now that you're over your little hurt feelings, are you gonna go for her again?"

I shook my head. "No, I'm gonna chill on that. She made herself clear that day in my office." I didn't mention the power move I'd pulled, making sure Gabi knew the invitation was still open.

"I'm surprised you're giving up so easy."

"I said I was chilling, not giving up. If something happens...it happens."

"Uh huh. Who is old boy walking up to her?" Dorian pointed to the "pretty boy" type who was approaching Gabi from behind.

"I don't know... but I'm about to find out."

----*Gabi*----

"So who is he?"

I turned to see Michael behind me, a smug grin on his face.

What the hell is he doing here?

I silently thanked God that he had approached me from the wrong the side to see Terrence kiss me.

"I don't see how that's your business," I said shortly, turning on my heels to walk away.

"Hold on now." Michael grabbed my arm. "I came all this way to see you, and you're really gonna treat me like this?"

"Yes," I resisted the urge to snatch my arm away from him. He was exploiting the same thing he'd used on the plane. He knew I wouldn't make a scene. "I didn't invite you here, and I have no desire to talk to you."

"Your parents told me where to find you. They agreed that it would be a nice surprise."

"They lied. Let me go."

"Not until you dance with me." He pulled me forward as the band began to play again.

My knee twitched, begging to be shoved upward into his groin.

"*One dance*," I hissed at him, not bothering to hide the disgust on my face. "And that is *only* because I don't want to be embarrassed in front of my colleagues. But do not try me Michael. If you don't let me go after this song, I will claw your fucking eyes out right here in the middle of this dance floor without a second thought, reputation be damned."

He ran his hands over my backside. "You are *so* sexy when you get upset Gabi."

"Keep your hands on my waist. High on my waist," I demanded, rolling my eyes.

"So you didn't answer my question."

"What question?"

"Who was that you were dancing with. It looked...cozy."

"Who, Whitaker?" I hoped that using his last name would dispel suspicion. "He's a coworker."

"Just a coworker?"

"Not that it's any of your business, but yes, just a coworker," I snapped.

I was annoyed with myself for letting him get under my skin, but I was even more annoyed that my parents had the nerve to send him to me. They knew how I felt about him, knew I would never marry him, yet they insisted on shoving him in my face. As soon as the song ended I pulled away, the scowl on my face daring him to try anything.

He followed me as I walked away. "Can I give you a ride home?"

"Mike, get real. You really think I want you knowing where I live? Besides, the firm has a driver, that's how I got here, it's how I'll get back, thanks."

"Gabi, come on. Stop acting like this."

"I could say the same for you. Why are you acting like me hating your guts is new information? Didn't we text about this two months ago? Just leave me alone, please."

Where the hell is Regina?

I walked away, hoping that he wouldn't follow this time. Glancing back, I was relieved to see that he was still in the same spot, watching me. Just that short interaction with him had drained my energy. I was glad to see that the event was winding down, and people were starting to leave. An uneasy feeling washed over me as I headed for the door, and I looked up to see that Michael had moved to the front doors, still staring at me.

It occurred to me that he might follow me, and I had no idea what I could do to prevent that.

"So who's the Michael Ealy look alike?"

"Not now Terrence," I snapped, turning to look at him.

"Whoa, sorry." He raised his hands in defeat. "I'm just messing with you, Gabi. What's wrong?"

I gave a heavy sigh. "The doppelganger is my ex, Michael. I wasn't expecting him to be here, and I'm a little on edge about it. Sorry for snapping at you."

"So he looks like the guy and they have they same name. That is...interesting."

"Terrence, don't-"

"Ok, ok. You seem more than just a *little* on edge though. You were very relaxed when I left you," he said, winking as he flashed his sexy smile at me.

"Yeah, he noticed."

"So? You said he was an ex right?"

"It seems like he hasn't gotten the memo."

Terrence stepped closer, grabbing my hands. "Ahh, this is the ex your parents like? Do we need to give him a show?"

"No." I gently pulled my hands away, not wanting Michael to see. "But, you can give me and Regina a ride home, if your sister doesn't mind. I don't want him following us."

"That's not gonna keep him from following you. Let me go have a little talk with him."

"Absolutely not, that would just egg him on." I bit down on my lip, trying to think of a solution.

"I can just take you to my place." Terrence offered, a suggestion that I answered with rolled eyes.

"There is *no way* I'm spending the night at your house. And what about Regina?"

"Gabi, I'm not gonna try anything with you. Yeah, I've flirted with you tonight, because I like you. I have a guest bedroom that my sister uses when she wants to be in the city, but she's going home with Neil. Dorian will get Regina home safely. There's a nice bed, a TV, and an attached bath. You can lock yourself in, and you wouldn't even have to look at me. I'll drive you home in the morning."

"No more flirting?" I asked. The longer I felt Michael's eyes boring into my face the more desperate I was to just get out of there, and away from him.

"No more flirting," Terrence assured me.

"Let me go talk to Regina, then please, get me out of here."

GABI

My phone rang bright and early, at 7am. I wasn't surprised at all to see my mother's name and number on the screen. I knew I saw the look on Michael's face when the valet pulled up in Terrence's car, and he helped me into the passenger seat, that he was going to call my parents to "snitch" on me.

I was groggy, still buried underneath the bed linens. "Hello?"

"What on earth is your problem?" my mother asked angrily from the other end of the line.

"Mother dear, whatever do you mean?" I asked sarcastically.

"Poor Michael called us nearly in tears last night, saying that you had refused him and gone home with another man!"

Poor Michael? Oh my God.

"That sounds about right, mom."

"That boy is never gonna stick around with you treating him this way!" my mother exclaimed.

"That's...kinda the point. I *want* him to go away."

"You don't know what you're saying, dear. I guess you two

are having some sort of lover's spat, but you'll come back together. Gabrielle, you know your father expects you to marry Michael. He'll provide an excellent life for you."

I sighed heavily into the speaker. "It's been 8 months since I broke up with him, mother, and I'm not interested in going back. At all. When are all of you gonna get that? Living with a cheater and borderline abuser isn't a good life."

I still remembered the night of our breakup as vividly as if it'd happened last night.

———

"What do you mean?"

I put my hands on my hips, annoyed that he was acting so clueless. "I mean exactly what I said, Michael. It's over. I'm moving to Atlanta in two months, and I'm not taking this baggage with me."

"I can't believe you're still thinking about movi--"

"Not thinking about. I am. I just sent my new roommate my deposit and first month of rent."

He stood, trying to grab me at the waist to pull me closer. "Why are you doing this?" He still thought he had that hold on me, that I would just melt into his arms and do what he said. Not anymore.

"Because I'm tired of this, Michael. I'm sick of being told what to do, I'm sick of living with my parents. I'm sick of the bougie, fake ass people that my parents seem to love, I'm sick of Chicago, and Michael... I'm just really fucking sick of you."

"You just need a little down time. Hit the spa, take some time off."

I shook my head. That was his answer every time I was upset with him. A day at the spa.

"I got my bar results today. I passed, and I'm moving to Atlanta. I'm going to be a lawyer, and I happen to think I'll be a good one. Who knows, maybe I'll even find myself a new man."

That got his attention.

"Don't joke with me about that. You let another man touch you and I'l--"

"You'll what, Michael? It's fine for you to have your 'hoards of whores', but any mention of another man gets you all uptight."

"Hoards of whores? Gabi, you're too beautiful to be talking like that. This cursing and stuff is gonna have to stop before we get married."

"Are you fucking deaf? Why are you still talking about a wedding that's never gonna happen? No. You know what, I'm done trying to explain this shit to you. I'll see you around, Michael, or not. Hopefully not. Goodbye."

I picked up my purse and keys from the counter, turning to leave. A pain in my arm stopped me just before my fingers reached for the doorknob. Michael was gripping me just below the shoulder, so hard that I thought my skin might break.

"Let me go!" I tried to pull away, but somehow his grip tightened as he pulled me back into the room, pushing me into a wall.

"You're not gonna talk to me like that and think there won't be consequences. Now you're gonna take your pretty little ass in the bedroom and wait for me. And get this Atlanta bullshit out of your head. It's not happe-"

He didn't get a chance to finish that statement before the lamp that had been on the table he pinned me beside went crashing into his head.

Mission accomplished. He let go of my arm to grab his head, doubling over in pain. The painting was next. I ripped it down from wall and chucked it, but he batted it away, lunging at me. Pain bloomed behind my eyes as my head hit the floor. Michael was on top of me, trying unsuccessfully to pin my arms down. I remembered that my keys were in my hand, and aimed for his, stabbing with all strength.

"Gabi, shit! My face!"

"I don't care about your damn face, are you crazy?" I maneuvered the pepper spray that was attached to the keys into my hand. "What *on earth made you think you could put your hands on me? I'm not one of your little sluts, I don't think you hung the moon. You put your hands on me like that again, and I will kill you. Got it?"*

I didn't wait on an answer. I grabbed my purse and got the hell out of his house.

————

"Oh honey, don't be dramatic," my mother said, with an annoying little laugh.

What?!

"How is wanting someone to be faithful and not put their hands on me being dramatic?"

"You act like the man was bringing home babies and putting you in the hospital!"

"Oh, should I have waited until then?" I asked in disbelief.

"Gabi, listen to me sweetheart. If you want a good man like Michael, you're gonna have to curb this little rebellious streak of yours. Learn that sometimes, to keep your husband happy, you have to put up with things you don't like. That's just the way it is if you want someone to take care of you." She said it so simply, as if she were sharing a cookie recipe.

"I *don't* want a man like Michael, mom. I want someone who respects me enough to treat me well, and he's not it. We're not just talking about watching too much football, or leaving socks on the floor. And I don't need anyone to take care of me, I just started a great career. I'll be taking care of myself."

"On that little *lawyer* salary?"

"Yes, actually. It's plenty. I'm not like you mom, I don't have to have designer clothes, a fancy car, any of that. When I get married, I just want to be happy." I fought to keep the tears that were forming in my eyes from coming through in my voice. I'd been having this exact same conversation with my mother every month since Michael and I broke up, and I was getting tired of it. I couldn't understand why my parents were so oblivious, and why it didn't matter to them that Michael had mistreated me.

"That's just a passing fantasy sweetheart. You need to be realistic about your future."

"Why do you think I moved to Atlanta? This is one of the best places for my career, mom."

"Oh, God, you're really serious about this law thing?" She didn't hide the contempt in her voice.

"What? Mom, why would you and dad spend all of that money sending me to college, and law school if you didn't think I was serious?"

"Well after you wouldn't give in when we threatened to take away your trust fund, we figured you just needed to get it out of your system. Besides, we had to bring something to the table if we wanted Michael and his parents to really consider you a suitable match."

I dropped the phone into my lap, grabbing a pillow to muffle the frustrated scream that I let out, then counted to ten several times before I picked up the phone again.

"Gabi, darling, are you still there?"

"Yes, mother. I'm here," I said shortly. "Did you guys seriously only put me through school to make me more *eligible*? Is that what you're telling me?"

"It's exactly what I'm telling you."

"I've gotta go. I'll talk to you later." Not bothering to wait for a response, I ended the call, and then flopped back onto the pillows. It wasn't until Terrence knocked on the door a few seconds later that that I remembered I wasn't even in my own apartment.

"Gabi, you ok?" he asked through the door.

Crap, he must have heard that scream.

"Yeah," I replied.

"You want some breakfast?"

"Sure, thanks."

I climbed out of the bed and went into the bathroom to brush my teeth and wash my face before I exited the bedroom and made my way into the kitchen. Forcing a smile to my face, I brushed away thoughts of the conversation with my mother and sat down at the counter, watching Terrence as he moved around the kitchen in a fitted tank and basketball shorts.

Damn he looks good.

"Good morning," he tossed over his shoulder.

"Good morning to you too."

He turned around, a huge smile on his face as he placed the breakfast he seemed to be working so hard on in front of me. I quickly clamped a hand over my mouth, trying to suppress the shout of laughter that bubbled up, but it was in vain.

"Oatmeal, Terrence?! All of that chopping and stirring and sweating you were over there doing, but you just handed me a bowl of oatmeal!"

"You don't like oatmeal?"

I glanced up at him as he put his own bowl down beside mine. "No, I love oatmeal. I hope I don't seem ungrateful, that just threw me for loop."

Let me show you a secret," he said, reaching over me to grab my spoon. "If you go ahead and stir it, you'll see the raisins, apples, and walnuts in the bottom. That's what the chopping and stirring was about. I know that's upside down, but it still tastes the same."

Damn he smells good.

"This is much better than the little instant packets I usually eat." I smiled at him, still grateful that he'd rescued me the night before, despite how awkward the last few weeks had been between us.

"You eat that trash?"

"I do," I admitted, shaking my head. I watched him out of the corner of my eye as we ate. Since we met, I'd wanted to stroke the velvety hair of his beard. Sitting here, sharing a meal with him, that urge was stronger than ever, intensified by the sight of his biceps flexing every time he moved. I tore my eyes away, suddenly remembering the comment he'd made the night before.

"I'm in the group that wants to take you home and take that dress off of you."

I shivered at the thought.

"Are you ok?" Terrence was looking at me, concerned.

"What? No. I'm fine. Perfectly fine."

----*Terrence*----

DON'T PRY, she'll talk about it when she wants to, if she wants to.

I had to keep telling myself that as I stood beside Gabi, drying off the clean dishes as she passed them to me. Her red-rimmed, puffy eyes said she'd been crying before she came out for breakfast, but she claimed to be fine.

"Thank you for letting me stay here." She pulled the stopper from the sink as she handed me the last pot. "And letting me use your towels, and your sister letting me use her clothes, and finding a new toothbrush for me. You wouldn't even let me do the breakfast dishes by myself, so I owe you."

"You don't owe me anything Gabi. The toothbrush came from the stuff my 'extreme couponing' aunt is always bringing over. I have plenty of towels, and a washing machine, so that's not a problem either. And about the clothes, my sister lost so much weight when she was sick that it's gonna take her some time to fit that stuff again. Trust me, you haven't put me through any trouble." I folded the towel I'd used to dry the dishes. From the inquisitive look on her face, I knew she wanted to ask about Tarryn, but she didn't push it.

"Still. I just want you to know that I appreciate it."

"I know. You're welcome."

"So I need one last favor."

I groaned, letting out a heavy sigh as I tossed the towel down on the counter. "What is it *now*, Gabi?" I teased.

"Ohhh, don't be like that. Do you think you could go ahead and drive me home now?"

"Yeah. I was actually just about to ask you. You got some gas money?" I led the way to the front door, where I slipped on my shoes.

She raised her eyebrows, caught off guard by the question. "Uhh, yeah. We'll have to stop at an atm, and I ca-"

"Gabi, did you think I was serious?" I chuckled at the serious expression on her face, wondering what was weighing so heavily on her mind that she couldn't take a joke.

"No, but I didn't wanna be embarrassed in case you were." She laughed as she pushed her hair back from her face. She'd taken her hair down from the style she'd worn to the charity event the night before, and it was a mess, but it reminded me of how she'd worn it the first day we met. Even with messy hair, in borrowed, oversized clothes, Gabi looked beautiful.

It was all I could think about as I drove her home.

TERRENCE

I watched in confused silence as Gabi stormed into my office. She flung the door closed behind her and started pacing, mumbling under her breath as she got more and more worked up. She was so upset that she didn't even see me sitting there. I wanted to speak up, alerting her to my presence, but I knew she would be embarrassed that I had seen whatever this was.

Suddenly, whatever dam had been holding back her tears broke, and she was standing in the middle of my office, sobbing. I rushed over to her, pulling her chin up as I wiped tears from her face.

"Oh God, Terrence?" She cried harder. "I thought you were still in court, I didn't want anybody to see this."

"What in the world is going on?" I stepped back to give her some room.

"It's stupid. I don't even know why I'm so upset about it."

"Gabi, that's a whole lot of tears for something stupid. Tell me what's going on."

"Mock Trial."

"Ohhhh. I see."

I had forgotten that Gabi was participating in the Mock Trials at the firm. It was rare for a first year, but she had put her name in the ring, and earned her spot in the finals through a "tournament" of trials, just like the other associates. Just like Dana, who was the most cutthroat attorney I'd ever met. Not just for a third year associate. Period.

"That *bitch* Dana!"

Oh, shit.

She started pacing again. "She's *such a bitch*. How can anybody be such a bitch?"

"What did she do?"

"She came to me yesterday, after we had gotten our case profile, offering to settle, which is perfectly acceptable, right?"

"Right," I responded, shaking my head. I already knew exactly where she was headed.

"I agreed to the terms. But when it was time to present it to Mr. Pritchard, who was acting as judge, that *bitch* acted like she had no idea what I was talking about. She tricked me!" Gabi stopped in front of me as she finished.

"If it makes you feel any better, she stole that move from a TV show."

She scowled as she started pacing again, obviously wound up. "It doesn't."

"I'm sorry you didn't win your case, Gabi...but you know that was a rookie mistake, right?"

She stopped in front of me again, the scowl still on her face. After a few seconds, it faltered, and tears broke through again. This time, I pulled her into my arms.

"That's why I'm so upset," she sobbed into my chest. "In the back of my mind, I knew I shouldn't trust her, but I thought I was being paranoid."

"There's no such thing as being too paranoid when it comes to your opponent, Gabi."

"I know," she said, sniffling. "I can't believe I messed up like that."

"It happens sometimes." I squeezed her shoulders before I stepped away from the hug. "But you should still be proud of yourself. You've been a lawyer for less than a year, but you kicked some pretty experienced ass to make it all the way to the finals."

"I lost because of a stupid mistake though. Ellen Atkins wouldn't have made this mistake," she said, referring to her idol.

"It's not the last one you're gonna make. Seriously, don't sweat it," I assured her.

"But the partners were all there, and-"

"Gabi," I interrupted. "You didn't cry in front of anybody else, did you?"

"No."

"Then trust me, they're impressed. I watched Dana make a guy who's been a lawyer for 20-something years break down in court one day. She's ruthless, it's what she's known for."

"But-"

"But nothing. Listen, I know it's been a tough week for you. I wanna take you somewhere, guaranteed to boost your spirits. Is that ok?"

Gabi used her hands to dry the last of the tears from her eyes. "Will there be food?" "There will definitely be food," I replied, laughing. "I'll follow you to your apartment to drop your car off."

"Let's go."

THIS WAS DEFINITELY A MISTAKE. Why did I think this was a good idea?

I bit back a groan as Tarryn and my Aunt Rae exchanged sly smiles as soon as I walked through the kitchen door with Gabi. The look on their faces confirmed my suspicion that it had been wise *not* to let them know I was bringing a guest to dinner. A wedding ceremony would have been waiting for us if I had. They were practically radiating excitement as they waited to be introduced.

"Auntie, Sis, this is my *friend* and *coworker*, Gabi," I said, trying my best to keep a serious expression on my face as they both rushed forward, wiping dinner preparations from their hands. "Gabi, this is my Aunt Rae, and my sister, Tarryn." I couldn't help smiling as they both pulled her into hugs that were completely over the top for a first meeting. I hadn't introduced them to anyone since my high school prom date, so I guess they were giving Gabi all the hugs they'd built up over the years.

"I remember you from the breast cancer fundraiser last week," Tarryn said. "You're the young lady who spent the night with Terrence."

Aunt Rae grinned at me as Gabi blushed. "Spent the night?"

"Oh my God, not like that Auntie, we didn-"

"Hush, boy. Ain't none of my business anyway." She waved me off. "But I have heard that the best position for making babies is with the man on top-you know, if you were interested in something like that."

Is this really happening?

"You know, I've heard that before too Auntie," Tarryn chimed in. "And the woman needs to lay there for at least fifteen minutes for optimal chances of conception-if you needed to know that type thing."

"Really, y'all?" I turned to see that Gabi had her hand

clamped over her mouth, trying to suppress a laugh. "This is funny to you?"

"Yes," she replied, laughing. "They're just messing with you, but you're so serious."

"Gabi, they aren't playing."

"Yes we are." Tarryn put an arm around Gabi's shoulder. "We're just a little excited, because Terrence never brings anybody home. We're happy for the chance to embarrass him in front of his girlfriend."

"But I'm no-"

"You wanna help us with dinner, baby?" Aunt Rae asked Gabi, interrupting her. "It'll give us ladies a chance to get to know each other."

"Um, sure," Gabi agreed, shrugging in a gesture that said "why not?"

"Bye Ter-Bear." My sister shooed me out of the kitchen into the living room, where she cornered me.

"Ter...Bear?" I heard Gabi say, confused.

I massaged my neck, trying to work out the knot of tension that was building there. "Tarryn, you're killing me!"

"Mmmhmm. Spill it." She poked me in the chest as if she weren't almost a foot shorter than me.

"There's nothing to spill. I told you, that's my coworker. She had a rough week, and I figured a good meal, with good people should cheer her up some." I kept my voice low so Gabi wouldn't hear.

"Terrence, I saw the way you were looking at her at that event the other night. She is a lot more than a colleague to you. Let's not forget that you took her home with you!"

I shook my head as I looked down, focusing on a scuff in the polished hardwood floor.

"What's the problem?" Tarryn continued. "Would you get in trouble, get fired or something if you guys..."

"No, nothing like that, I don't think. Mr. Graham kinda

warned me against it, but not in 'you'd better not' way. More like 'it's not the best idea'. Maybe if I were her boss or something it would be a problem, but we're both associates, no ones cares," I explained.

"Ok, so what's the issue?"

"I just can't date a coworker, sis. I need to be able to focus on my job," I said, repeating the speech I frequently gave myself. "I don't like people in my business, and if those folks at the firm knew Gabi and I were dating, they would be *all in it*. And if it doesn't work out, then what? I'm getting looked at sideways by everybody because Gabi's crying all over the office. Word gets around that I can't be trusted with women, we start losing clients. The partners fire me, and I end up homeless, roaming the streets because nobody wants to hire the lawyer who can't be trus-"

"Terrence, shut up! That is the most ridiculous scenario I've ever heard!"

"I got a little carried away, huh?"

"You think?" she rolled her eyes. "Anyway, this could all be solved by keeping things professional when you're at work, not telling your coworkers that you're dating because it's not their business, and not screwing up, which means no messy breakup. Problems solved."

"It's not that simple, Tarryn."

"Yes it is, y'all are just being dumb." She turned on her heels and headed back to the kitchen before I could say anything else. I tried not to think about the fact that I actually agreed. Convincing Gabi was the problem.

————

"This is awesome." I scooped another forkful of food into my mouth. I usually ate simple meals, and a lot more takeout than I liked to admit, so this meal was exactly what I needed.

"Did you do something different with the macaroni?" I asked my aunt. "It's always good, but this is amazing."

"No, I didn't do anything different." A smile played at the corners of her mouth. "You should ask your girlfriend about it."

"Why should I ask Gabi about the macaroni?" I asked, confused.

"So you admit she's your girlfriend now?"

"Really, auntie?"

She took a sip of her sweet tea. "Well, you're the one who responded to me calling her that."

"She's the only person here besides you and Tarryn."

"Mmmhmm. Your lady friend made the macaroni, used up all of my nice cheese."

I looked over at Gabi, who was avoiding my eyes even though she had a big smile on her face.

"I had no idea you could cook. This is really good," I told her as I took another bite.

"Thank you." She smiled. "Before she died, I would spend summers with my aunt and uncle, and she was always cooking something. She taught me a lot, and they didn't have any kids, so they treated me like their own. We were really, really close. But...uh...there was a car accident, the day before I was gonna spend my last summer with them, before I headed off to college, so...yeah."

Her eyes were already shining with tears, and I wracked my mind for something to change the subject.

"So you were what, about 18? That's the same age Terrence was when their mom passed," Aunt Rae obviously wasn't catching the mental signals I was sending. "It was so hard for him to get past–"

"Auntie, I don't think she wants to talk about this." Tarryn glanced over at me. I wondered what she had read in my expression that made her come to my rescue. My aunt looked surprised.

"You're right sweetheart." She looked directly at me. "I'm sure *Gabi* doesn't want to talk about it."

After dinner, my sister and aunt pounced on Gabi again, leading her into the kitchen to help clean up, despite my protests. Declaring it "girl time", they kicked me out of the kitchen, and I headed out to the porch to relax until I was allowed back in.

"You look like you're really in the zone out here." Gabi stepped onto the porch. "What are you thinking about?"

"Nothing important. You having a good time?" I gestured for her to take a seat beside me on the wooden bench.

"I am," she replied. "Your aunt and sister are really sweet. I know this is probably weird, but they feel like family already. Is that weird?"

"Not at all, actually. I'm glad they made you feel comfortable. If they didn't like you, this would have been a very different visit."

"Well, I'm certainly grateful for that," Gabi said, laughing.

We sat in silence for a few moments before I felt her fingers brush against my arm, lifting up the sleeve of my t-shirt.

"This tattoo." She traced her fingers along the edges. "A cross, with a breast cancer ribbon. Jocelyn Whitaker. This is for your mom, isn't it?"

"Yeah. I got it the night of her funeral. I wasn't even thinking, just acting," I shook my head at the memory.

"It's beautiful. She must have been really, really important to you."

"She was," I admitted. "My biggest supporter, always smiling, always singing. And she used to make the *best* pecan pie in Georgia," I said, laughing.

She pulled her hand away to place them in her lap. "You miss her a lot, don't you?"

"...I do. My dad too." I cleared my throat, staring out at the stars that were beginning to appear in the dark sky.

"I'm sorry," she said. "I was just curious, since you've never mentioned it."

"Nothing to be sorry about. I usually don't like to talk about it, but you're good, really."

There was silence again, neither of us knowing what to say. When Gabi shivered, reacting to the increasing chill in the air, I immediately wrapped an arm around her, pulling her close. She tensed for just a moment, then relaxed, resting her head against my shoulder.

"Terrence?"

"Yeah?"

"...Thank you, for bringing me here. I needed this," Gabi said.

"You're welcome." I leaned over, placing a light kiss against the side of her forehead. "We've actually gotta get going though, so we can get some sleep. We've got court tomorrow."

"We? You mean you're not disowning me after my shenanigans today?"

"What?" I chuckled. "I told you, it's really not as bad as it might seem right now."

She lifted up her head, turning to look at me. "You're only saying that because you like me."

"No, I'm saying it because it's true. But I do like you," I admitted, meeting her eyes with mine.

"Terrence, don't do that," she said.

I let my gaze drift down to her lips. "Don't do what?"

"*That.*" She pulled back. "We shouldn't. You know that."

"And why the hell not?"

We both jumped in surprise at the sound of Aunt Rae's

voice, and turned to see her leaning through the open kitchen window behind us.

"Auntie, were you spying on us?" I asked, even though I already knew the answer.

"No, Tarryn was. I was just making sure she didn't miss anything," she replied, pointing to where Tarryn was probably standing, hidden behind the curtain.

"Y'all are a mess. Come on, Gabi. Let's go."

I held out my hand to help her up, and she accepted it with a smile. She was asleep by the time I pulled into the parking garage of her building, and instead of waking her immediately, I watched.

Why are you watching her sleep?

Why not? She looked completely at peace with her seat slightly reclined, and her body tucked against the door. It made me happy.

Damn. This might be a little more than a crush.

GABI

"So. You and Mr. Whitaker."

I kept my expression neutral under my uncle's watchful eye.

Could he possibly...?

"You'll have to elaborate, Uncle Bobby. Are you asking me a question, or...?"

I had no hopes of winning if the game was cryptic statements, but I could control it a little better if I nudged him toward his point.

"I think you know. You're a lawyer, Gabi. Read between the lines."

I should have known he wouldn't make it easy.

"He and I get along fine. He can go a little overboard with the work, but it's nothing I can't handle. I'm learning a lot." I busied myself cutting into my grilled chicken, very aware that my uncle was still watching, waiting on something to betray the fact that I wasn't telling the whole story.

Uncle Bobby took a sip from his water. "You left the gala with him last week. And apparently, spent the night at his house."

Damn.

I shoved a forkful of salad into my mouth and maintained my poker face. I carefully chewed and swallowed, then took my own sip before I answered. "Yes. That happened."

"May I ask what you and Mr. Whitaker did in his condo?"

"Are you asking as my uncle, or my boss?"

"Both."

I sat up a little straighter, looking him directly in the eyes. "I slept, had an unpleasant phone call with my mother, we had breakfast, and then he took me home."

"Is that all?"

"Yes."

He sat back in his chair, appearing to choose his words carefully before he spoke. " As your uncle, I know that you're a smart, capable young woman. As your boss... I know we don't really have any anti-fraternization rules at P&G. But, as an adviser, if I may, I would strongly caution against anything other than a strictly professional relationship between you and Mr. Whitaker."

"Duly noted."

"Gabi..."

"Why are you pushing this so hard, Uncle Bobby? I can't have friends?" The question started out smug, but my heart dropped when I realized I had mistakenly revealed a little too much information.

"So you two are *friends* now?"

"Would it be a problem if we were?"

"Not at all. I think very highly of Mr. Whitaker. But, what would your parents and fiancé think?"

"I don't have a fi-- that's not funny," I scolded in response to my uncle's barely contained laughter.

"I'm just teasing, Gabi. How is Michael, by the way?"

After he got past the initial desire to commit murder, my uncle had been very amused by the results of Michael's attempt to intimidate me into obedience. My own parents, on the other hand, had not. They'd made the ridiculous demand that I apologize to him, and even went as far as covering the bill for the stitches he required to patch up his face. I smiled as I thought about the faint scar he still carried just underneath his left eye.

"At the moment? I don't know and don't care, but he's the reason I ended up leaving the gala with Terrence."

He listened as I recounted the events of the night, even the conversation with my mother.

"I just don't understand why they don't see Michael for who he really is," I finished, then took another bite of salad.

"Oh they see it, they just don't mind. From what you've told me, Michael is very much like your father."

Maybe he has a point.

They had the same arrogant, cocky attitude and quiet, but quick temper. The same need to control everything and everyone around them. The same lack of ability to be faithful. Hell, they even kind of looked alike, with their almond skin and sandy brown hair. And while I'd never seen it, I'd long suspected that my father didn't have a problem putting his hands on my mother if she put even a fraction of a toenail out of line.

The contrast between my father and my Uncle Bobby, who shared the same father, had always amazed me. As a child, I would sit awake at night in the beautiful purple bedroom my Aunt Pamela had set up for me at their house, wishing that instead of only being my "summer parents", they were just *mine*. I wanted so badly to live permanently in their comfortable home, where affection was given freely, from people whose love I never doubted. Instead, at the end of those 3 months of bliss, I would go back to a house where furniture was for viewing, not sitting, and I was constantly admonished about what I could do better. In my mind, my

Uncle Bobby and Aunt Pamela were warmth, light, and love, while my parents were a means to an end; a debt-free education, so I could get out of their grasp.

"Do you still miss her, Uncle Bobby?"

He looked surprised by my question, but the brightness in his eyes showed that he knew who I was referring to.

"Every single day, Gabi-girl. You don't love someone for 20 years and just forget."

I couldn't help the smile that crossed my face. Even though it had been almost 8 years since my aunt died in that car accident, Uncle Bobby still loved her. I was sure that he had dated other women since that time, but that type of love didn't go away.

"You know what I just realized? I've never heard the story of how you and Aunt Pam met."

He raised an eyebrow, and eyed me carefully across the table as he emptied his glass of water. Then, he shook his head, unable to suppress a grin. After I chastised him for a full minute about avoiding my question, he finally spoke, giving me an answer that I responded to with an audible gasp.

"We got paired together at work."

TERRENCE

"Come on Terrence, don't punk out on me."

I scowled at Dorian from my seat on the floor, watching as he screwed the faceplate onto the outlet we had just repaired.

"Man, kiss my ass."

"You're not gonna let this go, are you?"

"Hell no, I'm not gonna let it go. I got fucking electrocuted dealing with you."

"Stop exaggerating, it was just a little shock."

"That 'little shock' knocked me across the floor!" I stood, trying to shake the slight tingle that still lingered in my arms and legs. I should have known that Dorian's latest adventure in DIY home repair wouldn't end well for me. They never did. In the year since Dorian had purchased this house, I had fallen from ladders, almost lost a finger to a saw, and spent weeks in pain after straining my back helping him build a fence.

"You're fine. Did you forget I was a doctor?"

"How could I? You remind me every chance you get."

"Whatever man. When is your next little date with

Gabi?" Dorian passed me a beer from the cooler then leaned onto the counter as we admired our work. Despite the mishaps, I had to admit that with my help, the foreclosure was starting to look like a home again.

"They aren't dates. It's not even like that."

"Are y'all still avoiding the obvious?"

"I don't know what you're talking about, D."

That was a lie. I knew he was referring to the fact that in the month since I'd taken Gabi to meet my aunt and sister, we'd spent most of our free time together. We'd spent Saturdays at movie matinees, had Sunday dinners with my sister and aunt, been to concerts, played pool, and shared countless meals with each other. Platonically. There was an unspoken rule of no hand holding, definitely no kissing, and we took care to only be alone together in my office, where neither of us was willing to take the risk of being caught again.

"Oh, ok. I'm glad to hear it's not like that. I mean, I wasn't gonna say anything, but Gabi's not really *that* special for you to spending *all* your time with like that. She's pretty, *I guess*, but I don-"

My nostrils flared as I interrupted him. "You don't even know her, D, talking about 'she's not special'. How the hell would you know? She's smart, driven, funny, sweet, and she's fucking gorgeous."

Dorian smirked at my clenched fists. "So what exactly were you saying about it 'not even being like that'? Cause it sounds pretty 'like that' to me."

Shit.

I took a long swig from my beer, then scrubbed a hand across my face. "I'm confused, man, " I blurted out, then took another drink. "It's like, I know I shouldn't date a coworker. I know it's a bad idea, just drama waiting to happen. Mr. Graham even basically told me to stay away from her, but D, I *can't*. I don't know what the hell is wrong with me."

"Ah, see this is where avoiding girlfriends all your life is about to bite you in the ass. You're just catching feelings, it's not a big deal."

"I'm *not* in love with her D."

"Nobody accused you. I'm not saying you're *that* far gone, but you like her a lot more than this 'friendly co worker' crap you're trying to convince me of. We've been homeboys since kindergarten, dude. I *know* you. When have you ever thought about a chick longer than a week? Never. And you haven't even slept with her! Are you really gonna stand here and tell me this is normal for you?" Dorian shook his head as he finished his beer.

I couldn't deny it. This was definitely outside of the norm for me, because I'd never kept anyone woman around long enough to have this problem. Maybe it was just the close proximity. We were forced to spend countless hours together, so it was only natural that we would develop these feelings. But I wasn't sure it even mattered how it happened. Only *that* it happened, and I couldn't do anything about it.

GABI

I couldn't stand how much I missed him. It was disgusting, really. It was only the second day of his four-day trip to Birmingham to meet a client with that *bitch* Dana and Uncle Bobby, but sitting in his office all day made his absence even louder. I was lonely.

"This isn't working!" I snapped the file closed, and then threw my pen down on top of it, frustrated. How was I supposed to work when I couldn't get my mind of Terrence? Of course, that's exactly why I needed to *get my mind off of Terrence.* But that wasn't happening any time soon.

You are completely crazy.

That realization didn't stop me from rounding the desk to sit in his chair. I settled back into the leather, smiling when I realized it still held the faint scent of his cologne. It made me feel like he was close. I *always* felt good when I was close him, and I made it a point to do so as often as I could. It was a secret pleasure of mine.

With Michael, I had never felt completely at ease. There was always a need to look perfect, act perfect, *and be* perfect. With Terrence, I could sit around in a messy ponytail, drip mustard on my shirt, or pig out on pizza, and not feel self-conscious at all. He didn't expect me to be anything other than *me*, and it was glorious.

My thoughts were interrupted by the rumbling of my stomach, and I decided that it was time for lunch. There was a nice little Cajun restaurant in the building next door to ours, and I made up my mind that a bowl of gumbo was exactly what I needed to lift my lonely little spirits for the day.

My bowl had been in front of me for less than five minutes when someone sat down across from me.

I put my spoon down, crossing my arms in front of my chest as I looked up. "What do you want, Josh?"

He smiled at me as the waitress delivered him a drink and a plate of food, waiting until she was gone to speak. "What, a man can't eat lunch with a pretty colleague?"

"It's what you might want other than lunch that has me worried."

He cocked an eyebrow at me and grinned. "Well, Ms. Jacobs, if that's what you want, I can certai-"

"Ew! You know that's not what I meant!

"Relax, I'm joking."

"It's not funny."

Josh threw his hands up in defeat. "Hey, I see that now. Won't happen again."

Not wanting my food to get cold, I picked up my spoon, and we talked while we ate. To my surprise, Josh wasn't quite as slimy as I thought. He was smart, and funny, and I was actually enjoying myself, until he finally dropped the bomb I was sure he had been holding since he decided to sit down.

"So, you and Terrence."

Here we go.

"Are you two an item?"

"No," I said, taking a sip from my sweet tea. "We're not. What gave you that impression?"

"Well, you seem to spend a lot of time with him, so I thought maybe you guys had a 'thing'."

"A thing? No, nothing like that. Terrence just happened to be one of the first people my age that I met in Atlanta. The other was my roommate, so that's who I spend my time with. He's a friend." It wasn't exactly a lie. It was actually completely true. All I did was leave out the fact that I liked him, in a completely non-friendly way.

"So when can I take you out to dinner? As a friend, of course."

"I'm gonna go with never. Did you forget about Dana?" As much as I disliked his girlfriend, I wasn't about to get on her bad side about *her* man. I had seen what she could do in the mock trial, and I had no interest in seeing what she was capable of when there were real consequences.

"No, but I'm trying to. We broke up a few weeks ago."

"Good for you, but still, no," I said, pushing away my now empty bowl. I wasn't about to be seen as his rebound girl. I didn't even want him!

"You let Terrence take you out to dinner."

"Terrence has *never* 'taken me out to dinner', we've grabbed Chinese while we were working on a case, ordered pizza, stopped to get lunch. It's not the same thing. Besides, I spend close to 60 hours a week with him, I know he's not going to do anything inappropriate."

Now that was definitely a lie. I spent at least half of my time with wondering when he would kiss me again. Not *if*. When. The difference was that I wouldn't *really* mind a little impropriety from Terrence, even though I knew it wasn't a good idea. However, the thought of being kissed or touched by Josh disgusted me. Who knows where his lips and hands had been?

"So you've gotta spend some professional time with me first. Ok. How about lunch again next week, on me? That is, if your *little boyfriend* Terrence doesn't mind."

So he wasn't gonna let it go.

"Do you really think there's something going on with he and I?"

"I will if you won't even go to lunch with me. That would mean those rumors were true, and you're just giving me lip service about him being your 'friend'." He pushed away his plate and sat back, resting his hands in his lap as he waited for me to respond.

"I know manipulation when I see it," I said, careful to keep my tone playful. "But if it will quell your little office gossip, whatever, I'll go to lunch with you. *Just* lunch."

———

"Again?"

I raised an eyebrow at Terrence, annoyed.

"Why do you say "again" like that?" I glanced away as I zipped my purse closed. "Like it's a problem?"

"It's not a problem." He looked up from his laptop then, wearing an expression that very clearly contradicted his words.

"The look on your face says different."

"I don't have an issue with you going to lunch with Josh. Not at all," he said, quickly clearing the annoyance from his face.

He was lying, or at the very least, pretending. Despite his protest, I knew that it bothered him that I had accepted Josh's invitation to lunch, again. When Terrence returned from Alabama, I'd told him about the encounter with Josh. He didn't say very much about it, just laughed when I shared that I'd agreed to a second lunch. When he found out that I'd been invited to a *third* lunch, he'd given me a gruff "oh" and gone back to his work. Since then, he was noticeably different. Less talk, no play, and definitely no 'friendly' outings. Now, on the fourth lunch, it seemed we were finally going to address... whatever this was.

"Then why have you been acting pissy since I started spending time with him?"

"Nobody is acting pissy, Gabi, I'm just trying to be professional, remember?" he asked. His expression was cold as he looked back to the computer.

I narrowed my eyes at him, biting back the urge to make a smart comment. It was true, he had never technically been impolite, or anything that even bordered on rude, but still. Compared to the warm hugs and long talks I had gotten used to, his new attitude was like a slap in the face.

"Of course I remember," I snapped, snatching my purse off of the desk and swinging it up onto my shoulder as I stomped out of the office.

I don't even like Josh like that. I like you, dummy.

I ignored the people in the halls as I made my way to the elevator, hoping to reach my car without having to talk to anyone. Uncle Bobby was at Vanessa's desk when I walked past, but luckily, they were deep in conversation so I got away with fake smile and a wave. I released a deep breath that I hadn't even realized I was holding as the cold metal doors started to slide closed.

Damn.

A hand slid between the doors just before they met, triggering them to open again. I closed my eyes, trying to fight back tears as Josh stepped onto the elevator.

"Hey, were you headed to meet me at the restaurant?" He flashed a smiled as he stepped toward me.

"No, actually," I shook my head. "I was getting ready to

text you, but I really just need a little time to myself, so I'm gonna have to cancel today, sorry."

"Aww man. You need somebody to help cheer you up?" He took a step toward me, stretching his arms toward me in an invitation to embrace.

"Uhh, no. No thanks," I replied, waving him off as I eased back.

Just leave me alone, damn.

"Oh, you're gonna act like that now? Your loss."

I rolled my eyes as he made a big display of adjusting his tie, then the Rolex on his wrist.

There the sliminess is. I knew he couldn't suppress it too long.

I didn't even bother responding, just thanked God when the elevator finally reached the ground floor, finally releasing us into the parking garage. I quickly made it to my car, where I climbed in and made a fast escape to my apartment so that I could have some peace.

I flung myself across the bed, wondering what was wrong with Terrence. He was always the one pushing the boundaries, constantly in my face, taking me to meet his family, but all of a sudden he wanted to be 'professional'. There was no good reason for him to treat me any different than the friend that I *thought* I was to him. We had been working together well, and having a great time, until of all the apparently awful things I could do, I'd had lunch with Josh.

Why should he even care who I had lunch with? We weren't even dating, let alone serious. I was sure he was probably screwing around to his single heart's content when he wasn't around me, but I have *lunch*, and it's a problem. This entire situation was exactly why dating coworkers was a bad idea. Unnecessary drama.

TERRENCE

D amn it.

I closed my eyes, running a hand over my face as the door closed behind Gabi. I knew I should have just kept my mouth closed, but that "again" had slipped out before I could catch it. She was free to see who she wanted, but I would be lying if I said it didn't bother me that she had chosen Josh.

You lied when she asked you if there was a problem though.

I did. But there was no reason for me to spread my frustration to Gabi. She's a smart girl, perfectly capable of determining what she wants. And if that happened to be Josh...I couldn't really do anything about that. It didn't keep me from imagining my fist connecting with his jaw though. Every time they got back from lunch, he had an annoying smirk on his face like they had a secret. As if lunch wasn't the only thing that had been on the menu.

He even hinted at it to me. Little comments about her being sexy, wild and sweet, delivered with a wink. It had taken everything in me not to choke his ass that day. But Gabi would come prancing back in, all smiles, like nothing happened.

How could she entertain his bullshit? I hated to admit it, but Josh was a cool guy. Charming. It's what he was known for, charming women right out of their panties. I shook my head, trying to prevent that thought from being seared into my memory.

Why was she even out with him? After all of that talk about being professional, not dating co workers, she went out with *him*. It... shit, it hurt.

I laid my head down on my desk, feeling exhausted. This was throwing me for a loop. How did I go from planning the spacing of one night stands to being jealous that a girl I'd never slept with was sharing a meal with someone? I hated that Dorian was right. I was definitely 'catching feelings', as he'd called it.

I popped my head up as my laptop chimed, notifying me that I had an email.

"Mr. Whitaker. I need you in my office, ASAP. I need to talk you about something *now*." - Robert Graham.

That didn't sound good.

----*Gabi* ----

I turned the corner just in time to see Terrence leaving Uncle Bobby's office. Everything about him looked pissed off, from his tense body language to the scowl on his face. He walked right past me, not looking at me or saying a word. My original motives forgotten, I took the last few steps to the office, knocking on the door before I walked in.

"Gabi-girl, to what do I owe this pleasure, in the middle of the day?" Uncle Bobby smiled up at me from his desk.

"Well, I was coming to talk to you about something, but

what's going on with Terrence? He looked really upset coming out of here."

"Oh, I just told him that one of *your* mistakes on a legal document very nearly cost one of our clients close to a million dollars."

Everything went black for a few seconds. When I opened my eyes again, the room was blurry, and everything sounded muffled.

"What?" I choked out as clarity came flooding back, and I really registered what he'd said.

"Yes, you heard me right. I had to explain to him that it was *only* because one of the legal secretaries caught the error before it was sent over to opposing counsel that he still has a position here."

"But... if it was *my* mistake, why would-"

"Because you're his responsibility for this year, Gabi. If you mess up, he messed up. He understood that going in. His name is the one listed on the legal documents, not yours."

"But...I- That's not fair. Terrence is an amazing lawyer, you can't let something I did affect him like this! I can't even believe something slipped by me. I'm *meticulous* about making sure everything is in order, and then Terrence looks over it again before we have it sent to the other side, so-I." I swallowed over and over, trying desperately to wet my dry throat as tears sprang to my eyes for the second time that day. I couldn't believe Terrence had gotten reprimanded over my mistake. "What was it?" I asked.

"What was what?"

"The mistake, Uncle Bobby."

"Oh, that. There was no mistake." He grinned down at the documents that were scattered across his desk.

"...What?"

"There wasn't a mistake. I said I *told* him that, not that it actually happened." He glanced up at me with a smile. "I probably shouldn't tell you this, since you work so closely with him, but we're about to allow Terrence to enter the partner training program. He's only about to be on his fourth year, but he's ready. You *cannot* tell him about this though." He was still wearing a big grin as he told me all of this, not noticing the confused look on my face.

"...What?" I asked again.

"It was a test, Gabi," Uncle Bobby explained, putting his pen down. "I needed to know if Terrence would throw you under the bus. You're already proving your potential to be a great attorney, but you're still a first year associate. You're still green, you're supposed to mess up. He could have easily tried to shift blame to you, but instead, he owned up to his mistake. He accepted responsibility when he needed to, and *that,* my dear, is admirable. It let me know the kind of man he is, and that he's ready to move forward here."

"That's great, but he thinks I almost cost him his job!" I exclaimed. I wanted to sweep my arms across his nice mahogany desktop, knocking the contents to the floor. How could he sit there so calmly, delivering this news with a smile on his face? I couldn't imagine what Terrence must be thinking, how angry he probably was with me.

"Don't worry about that. It's just a little rite of passage that every associate before him has had to go through as well. He'll find that out soon enough, and in the meantime, he'll still be absolutely professional with you. Trust me."

I wasn't so sure.

———

I WAS DREADING HAVING the face Terrence. First, the whole misunderstanding with Josh, and now this "almost fired" nonsense. Was God trying to tell me something? I hovered outside of the door to Terrence's office, trying to think of an excuse not to go in.

With a relieved sigh, I remembered that I had a large file in my bag that we needed a second hard copy of. Sure, I could just print it, but I welcomed a reason to burn 15 minutes in the copy room. It was tucked out of the way, and always empty, so I knew it would be quiet. I headed that way, pausing as the door was opened from the other side.

Ughhhh, could this day get any worse? Any?

"Just the beautiful girl I wanted to see." Josh stepped forward with a smile, pulling me at the waist. I quickly wiggled out of his grasp.

"Josh, get off of me." I crossed my arms over my chest, disgusted by the way his eyes were roving over my body. "Can you move?"

"Gabi, you don't have to do this "hard to get" shit with me. You think I haven't been picking up your vibes?" He grabbed my backside with both hands as he lowered his mouth to mine. It took me a second to recover from the shock that he was bold enough to touch me like this, in plain view for anyone that came along.

"Get your damn hands off of me!"

"Shit, shit! Gabi, shit, stop!"

I had started hitting him, open-handed slaps to the face that were resonating through the empty hall.

"Don't you ever touch me again, or I swear, I will claw your fucking eyes out, do you hear me?" I hissed, taking a step forward. "Don't even look my way, ok?" I turned on my heels and stomped down the hall into Terrence's office, forgetting that I was trying to avoid him.

He looked up when I walked in, scowling before he turned his attention back to his work.

"Terrence...I-"

"Gabi, unless it's about this case, I really don't want to

hear it right now, ok? I'm not trying to be mean, I just wanna get this done- with no mistakes, if possible."

"I...ok," I replied, sitting down to pull my laptop out.

Can't blame him for being upset. I would be too.

-----*Terrence*----

I CRINGED at the look of hurt that crossed Gabi's face when I cut her off. I wasn't being fair, and I knew it. It really wasn't her fault that I hadn't reviewed the document carefully enough before submitting it. That was my problem, something I shouldn't take out on her. But after the way I'd just seen Josh gripping handfuls of her ass, I wasn't feeling particularly 'nice'.

All I'd wanted was extra paper from the copy room, but instead I'd walked right into a scene I could have gone my entire life without seeing. My little inkling of hope that it wasn't "like that" between her and Josh was gone, and it had taken any chances of me being friendly with it. From now on, the "professional" demeanor she was obsessed with was all she would get from me.

There was no music in Gabi's head today. She was still and quiet as we worked, making slow progress on the defense strategy for our clients. As soon as five o'clock hit, she was out of the door, mumbling something about working from home.

GABI

"Dang, are you still moping around?" Regina asked as she came in, with her hair tucked neatly under a slouchy knit hat. She unbuttoned her coat, then hung it by the door. "It's been what, a month since your little falling out with Terrence? I need you to get it together girl, you're dragging down the mood around here.

"I'm not moping, I'm just having a lazy day."

"Uh huh. Well, it looks like moping to me. I guess it's fair to say you two haven't made up?"

"Made up from what?" I crossed my legs as I sat up on the couch.

"From the whole Josh thing, then you almost getting him fired, duh."

"He still seems upset, so I'm just gonna leave it alone. I've only got about six more months working with him directly before I get to be on my own, so I can handle it," I replied.

"What makes you think he's still upset?"

"Well," I started with a sigh, "he's always harsh when he's pointing out any mistakes I make. He won't talk to me about anything that's not case related, and even when it *is* case related, he uses as few words as he possibly can. There's zero friendliness now."

"Oh, girl he has it *bad* for you," Regina replied as she sat down beside me on the couch. "You hurt his little feelings spending that time with Josh."

"That doesn't make any sense though, it was just lunch! And I didn't even like Josh like that, I was just being nice, and trying to slow down any rumors about me and Terrence. But you see how that turned out," I said, leaning back against the couch.

"Yeah, it bit you in the ass, didn't it?"

"I don't understand why he's mad though, it's not like he and I were together."

Regina cut her eyes at me. "Girl, because he likes you. Of course he got pissed off seeing you spending time with a male coworker after you told him *he* had to keep it corporate."

"It wasn't like that!"

"Yeah, but does Terrence know that?"

I didn't have an answer for that. He and I never discussed it, so he very well could think that Josh and I were more than we were. I was sure he'd noticed the abrupt end to our shared lunches, but he hadn't mentioned it, since we really weren't on speaking terms.

"Gabi, look." Regina placed a hand on my shoulder. "From what you've told me, Terrence is a really, really good guy, and you like him. Eventually, he's gonna come around, but in the meantime, you've gotta decide if you're gonna take that leap, see where the relationship leads. I know being cautious is your thing, but you're gonna have to ease off of that just a little."

"I know," I whined, laying my head down in her lap. Over the last six months, Regina had become like a sister to me, and I knew her advice was sound. She had a great job as a small business loan officer, a family and friends who loved her, this fabulous apartment, and a gorgeous doctor who adored her, even though she ignored him. Her life was awesome. If *anybody* could lead me on the right path, it would be her.

"But, it's not just being guarded. I could cost him a really important opportunity if my uncle doesn't like the idea of us dating. Maybe after he gets his promotion," I said, looking up at her.

"Fine. That puts a time limit on it for you to keep you from dragging this thing out. Hey, why don't you get dressed, and come see this movie with me? Fine ass Omari Hardwick is in it...," Regina said with a faraway look. "He is guaranteed to get your mind off of old boy."

"No, he actually *reminds* me of Terrence."

"Hmm. I guess I can see the resemblance. Barely. Maybe a little. But ok girl. We'll see something else. Now, come on, get moving. You're wearing a hole in the couch."

————

"I DIDN'T SAY your idea was stupid, Gabi."

"Yeah, but you implied it," I snapped, checking my cell phone for the time. It was nearly 10pm, and we'd been working on this defense strategy since 8am, only breaking for a quick lunch. I was tired, starving, and over it, but I knew we needed to at least come up with an idea.

"That's your own perception, Gabi, I don't have anything to do with that."

I crossed my arms over my chest. "Look, this is a waste of time. If we're just gonna argue, I can go home." I rolled my eyes as Terrence stood, and stalked over to the door, locking it.

"Neither of us is going anywhere until we get this work finished, so cut the attitude. We've gotta get this done." He stifled a yawn as he returned to his seat.

"You've gotta be kidding. *I* have an attitude? That's rich, Terrence."

We were seated on the same side of the desk, so I made a big show of turning my back to him. It forced me to confine myself to a small corner of the desk to work, but that was fine with me.

"Stop being childish, Gabi." He grabbed the arm of the chair to pull me back around to face him. "We have to work together on this, or we're gonna lose this case. And you know how you are about *losing*."

"What the hell is that supposed to mean?"

"That you can't handle losing. When Dana kicked your ass in Mock Trial, you ran in *my* office crying like a damn baby cause you lost." He turned back to the files in front of him, scribbling something in his barely-legible handwriting.

"I told you, I didn't even know you were in there. I was trying to be alone. I hope you didn't think I was looking for you to console me, because I can't *stand* you."

He didn't take his eyes off of the paper in front of him. "Yeah, right, you'd rather deal with the guy who'll chase anything wearing panties."

Heat immediately rose to my face at the reference to Josh. This was the first time he'd directly mentioned it, and he chose to bring it up like *this?*

"If I recall correctly, you were pretty damn jealous that it wasn't you," I snapped, narrowing my eyes at him.

"Yeah, and look at the bullet I dodged!"

"I... you... kiss my ass!" I stood up, flinging my chair away as I began gathering my things.

"You can't leave, Gabi!"

"Watch me!" I stormed over to the door, stopping short when I felt his hand around my arm, pulling me backwards. "Terrence, let me go," I warned, trying to shrug him off me. When that didn't work, rage took over and my fists went flying. He was going to let me go, one way or another. I did my best to lay out all of the anger, hurt, and confusion I'd been feeling over the last several months because of him.

"Damn it, Gabi, stop!" He snatched my arms at the wrist, trying to stop me from attacking him.

"Screw you!" I was still trying my hardest to get away, and maybe land a few more hits. He just held me tighter, pulling me so close that the only thing keeping us from touching was the steady grip he had on my wrists, which he placed against his chest.

"Gabi, I didn't mean that." He stared directly into my face until I made eye contact with him. My anger dissipated a little as we stood there, gazing at each other in silence. He leaned forward, kissing me softly against my lips. The room seemed to shift around me, and for a moment, I was at peace. In the back of my mind, this is what I'd secretly wanted, for him to just kiss me and make it all ok. But then I remembered all of his little dismissals, rude comments, and the pissy attitude he'd had toward me since my first lunch date with Josh.

I halfheartedly attempted to pull away, but he kissed me deeper, slipping his now-familiar tongue into my mouth, and my mind went blank. I didn't care about anything except how this kiss was making me feel. He released my wrists at the same time he ended the kiss, then tipped my chin upward so that I was looking at him.

"I'm sorry," he said, cupping the side of my face. "I shouldn't have said that, and I didn't mean it."

"Then why did you say it, Terrence?"

"Because, I...I don't know. Shit, because I'm confused!" He stepped back. "I like you, Gabi, more than I've liked anybody, ever. Knowing you were with him, hearing the stuff he would say about you, and seeing him touch you...it was just too much. It pissed me off, and I know I handled it badly. I really am sorry. You didn't deserve that."

"Seeing him touch me?"

"I saw you with him, outside the copy room."

"You didn't see what you thought you saw. It was *never* like between Josh and I. What you saw was him crossing a line, and if you'd stayed, you would have seen me smack the shit out of him," I replied. "I guess I could have made it clearer to *both* of you that I only saw Josh as a coworker. *Really*. Nothing more."

"Or I could have just not acted like a moody teenager." Terrence grimaced. I assumed he was remembering how coldly he'd been acting toward me since the whole thing with Josh.

"I get it. I probably would have felt the same way if it were reversed. I really like you too Terrence, but we're *not* supposed to be crossing that line," I said, thinking about what Uncle Bobby was planning for him. "But I would love it if we could go back to the way it was before."

"I'll take what I can get." He smiled as he pulled me into a hug.

"So you're not mad about me getting you in trouble?"

"I didn't even know you knew about that, but no, not anymore. I was *pissed* at first, but it really wasn't your fault that it got submitted with an error. I'm supposed to make sure, and I didn't. That's my bad, not yours."

"So we're good?"

"We're good."

———

"That's...different," Terrence said, eyeing my breakfast as he walked in.

"Trying to eat a little lighter these days," I replied, faking a cheerful smile. I had been frequenting a little bakery that served sausage, egg, and cheese sandwiches on the most heavenly biscuits I'd ever tasted. Unfortunately, my biscuit habit was beginning to show on my hips and thighs, and the abs I had worked so hard for between classes were long gone.

Terrence laughed as I scowled down at the scrambled egg whites and fruit I had gotten from the vegetarian restaurant across the street.

"You don't look happy about it."

"I'm *not* happy about it. But all of the eating out I've been doing is showing up on the scale, and I can't have that," I said, popping a grape into my mouth.

"I didn't know you were vain, Gabi." Terrence sat down across from me at his desk, a slight grin on his face as he unpacked his laptop.

"I'm not," I told him with a sigh. "But, I'll be going home for Christmas in a few weeks, and I know my mother is gonna be all over me about gaining weight."

"What? The only place you've gotten any bigger is your a-"

Terrence stopped as I raised an eyebrow at him, daring him to finish the statement.

"What I really wanna know is how *you* aren't flabby, with all of the takeout you eat," I said, taking the last bite of eggs.

"It's called exercise, my friend."

I scoffed at him. "And when exactly do you propose I do that? We're working 70 hour weeks around here most of the time!"

"You have to make time for it, if it's important to you. I hit the gym in my building whenever I can, 2-3am sometimes if I have to. I'm pretty serious about it," he said.

"I can tell." I stood to take my empty dishes to our break room. "Maybe I'll ask Regina if she wants to come work out with me today."

He leaned back into his chair to look at me. "I don't get an invitation?"

"Oh please, like you would want to come and work out with amateurs."

"I could help out."

"What, like, train me? Absolutely not."

"Why?"

"We would end up hating each other's guts."

"No we wouldn't."

"We totally would. You would go all super-trainer on me, and I'm not trying to have to curse you out," I said.

He grinned. "Wouldn't be the first time."

"That's true, but I was hoping I wouldn't have to do it again," I replied, with my hand on

the door knob. "I appreciate the offer, but no thanks."

"No problem. But, the offer stands."

I gave him another smile as I turned to walk out of the door. I would never, *ever* work out with him.

----*Terrence*----

"I CAN'T BELIEVE I let you talk me into working out with you." Gabi glared at me from her seat at the counter. It had been two weeks since she'd mentioned re-starting a workout routine, and I had finally convinced her to accept my offer of help.

I grinned, then passed her a cup.

"Drink that, or you're gonna hate me even more when you wake up tomorrow."

She raised the drink to her nose, then frowned in disgust.

"What the hell is this? It smells awful, like spoiled choco-late milk."

"It's a protein shake. Just knock it back as fast as you can, get it over with." I raised my own cup, and downed the shake. If she thought the smell was bad, the taste was likely to make her gag.

She was able to get it down, but gave me a dirty look afterwards, which I responded to with another grin. Between her and Regina, Dorian and I had been called every name in the book over the last hour, including some that I was sure they made up. Gabi had accidentally let the name of the track they were going to slip, and we had shown up just in time to talk them into spending their hour doing sprints and other strength training exercises. The squats were what had Gabi ready to kick my ass.

"I'm gonna kill you if I can't walk tomorrow."

"Oh, you'll be fine," I said, placing an arm around her shoulder as I walked up beside her.

"Whatever. I should be making you pay for a massage."

"Why pay, when I coul-"

"Terrence..."

I pulled her into a hug, savoring the scent of peaches and cocoa butter from whatever she'd showered with after our workout.

"You're gonna be ok, in a few days. Your legs just have to get used to it."

"Mmhmm." She responded, but she wasn't looking at me. Her eyes were on Regina and Dorian, who were sitting mere inches apart, having what appeared to be a very intimate conversation. There was lots of whispering, laughing, and touching. It was exactly the type of moment I wished I could have with Gabi.

"What are you thinking about?" Gabi asked, smiling up at me, but still not pulling herself away from my arms, which were still wrapped around her from the hug.

"Nothing you need to know. What are *you* thinking about?"

She lowered her eyes, but the pleased look remained on her face. "How much I appreciate you 'coincidentally' showing up at the track to help me today, even though I feel like I got a hit by truck."

I ruffled her hair, grinning when she smacked my hand away. "It was no trouble. I needed to work out anyway. Besides, you know I'll do anything for you girl."

Wow.

Gabi seemed un-phased by what I'd said, probably thinking it was just a throwaway comment between friends, but it wasn't. It was absolutely true.

GABI

I frowned down at the screen of my phone. The "call ended" message flashing there was staring up at me, partially obscuring a picture of Terrence and I at the gym. It was the second time I'd called him today, with no answer, and I definitely wouldn't be calling a third time. I didn't want to seem as if I was blowing him up, but I was worried. It was a Friday, but still a weekday, and it was totally unlike Terrence to not show up at the office, especially without letting me know. We didn't have anything on schedule for the day, but he would usually take this time to catch up on paperwork or do research for the next case.

I looked down at my phone again, wondering what to do. Terrence *never* ignored my calls. A quick glance at the screen told me it was after 5pm, so I began packing up to leave. The uneasy feeling I had about Terrence's absence kept gnawing at me, all the way down to my car. I sat at the wheel for several minutes before I made a decision about where to go. I just hoped I wasn't about to piss him off.

I TOOK A DEEP BREATH, trying to calm my nerves as my finger hovered over the doorbell to Terrence's apartment. Before I could lose my courage, I firmly pressed down and then released the button. As I waited, hoping he would open the door for my unannounced visit, I smoothed down the lightweight fabric of my maxi dress.

At least you look cute today.

That's right, I do look cute today, in my pretty coral dress and sandals. Hopefully cute enough that he'll actually open the door. Just as I was about to ring the bell again, the door swung open.

"Gabi, what's up?" he asked, a blank expression on his face. I wanted to answer, but for some reason, I couldn't seem to make myself speak. Terrence didn't look himself at all. He was wearing a tee shirt and basketball shorts that were clean, but wrinkled and he obviously hadn't brushed his hair or groomed his beard. Something was definitely off.

"Gabi?" he asked again, this time raising an eyebrow at me.

"Oh, um... I went to eat at Vortex, and I guess I wasn't thinking, and I ordered too much food. I was over here by your place, so I thought hey, maybe Terrence could eat this extra for me," I blurted out, stumbling over the words as I held up the to-go bag in my hand.

Terrence just stared at me for a moment before he shook his head. "You know I know you're lying, right? Vortex isn't anywhere near my place, and that bag has at least 3 plates in it."

"I may have embellished my story a little bit. Are you gonna invite me in?" I gave him my best pageant smile, swirling the bag of food at eye level in front of me.

He glanced behind him into his apartment, and then turned back to me with a strained expression on his face. "Uh..."

My hand flew up to my mouth as I gasped. "You have company?" I hadn't even considered that possibility before driving my eager behind halfway across Atlanta to come to his place. We had never discussed our sex lives, so even though I not-so-secretly hoped that he wasn't sleeping with anyone, I really had no idea.

"What? No." He raised an eyebrow at me again. "Why would I have anybody here? I just...wasn't expecting company, and my place is kind of a mess. But, you know I couldn't turn you away."

He stepped back, allowing me to walk into his apartment. I quickly deduced that the lack of fresh vacuum lines in the plush carpet and the few dishes in the sink had to be what he meant by 'kind of a mess', because nothing else seemed to be out of place. I was a bit obsessive about neatness and order too, and Terrence had a beautiful apartment, with finishes that screamed luxury. It was nice that he cared about main-taining it.

Yet another good thing about him.

But I wasn't supposed to be thinking about that. I was here to check on him. When I turned back to Terrence, he was standing at the sink, washing his hands so that he could eat. I was dying to know what he had been doing all day, but it didn't seem like the right time to ask.

We ate in silence. I snuck a few glances at Terrence as he devoured his food, and I noticed a distinct sadness in his eyes that made my heart ache in my chest. When he was done, he perched himself in front of one of the big floor-to-ceiling windows in his living room.

I approached him quietly, stopping when I was right beside him. When I glanced up, I was surprised to see that his eyes were wet. I reached over, intending to place a hand on his arm for comfort when my eyes landed on the tattoo he had gotten for his mother. As I looked down at the date that was inked below it, understanding washed over me. It was today's date.

"Oh, Terrence. I'm so sorry, I didn't mean to-"

"It's ok Gabi. I always just take the day off, keep to myself."

"No, it's not ok," I replied. "I was just worried when you didn't show up, and you weren't answering the phone. I really didn't mean to impose! I'm gonna go, you obviously wanted to be alone today."

"I don't." He grabbed my hand as I turned to walk away. "It's just what I'm used to doing. It's been ten years though. Maybe it's time to do something different. Stay?"

I allowed him to pull me into his arms and he hugged me close, planting a kiss on the top of my head. We stayed that way for a long time before he spoke.

"I think she would have liked you... a lot."

I pulled away slightly so that I could look into his face, but he was staring out of the window again, his eyes fixated on something I couldn't see.

"You actually remind me of her," he continued, finally glancing down at me. "Always singing and dancing to music in your head, constantly trying to feed me. Even the way you flex your fingers and scrunch your face up when you're super focused on something. Just little quirks, you know?"

I simply nodded, trying to keep my expression blank. I wasn't sure if I should let on how flattered I was that I reminded him of someone so important to him. He let me go and then turned away, subtly wiping his eyes.

Does he think I would tease him for crying about his mom?

"So." He cleared his throat before he changed the subject. "Do you wanna watch a movie with me or something?"

"Sure," I replied. He pointed in the direction of his couch, which was positioned in front of a large flat screen TV. As I watched, he pulled the cushions onto the floor and then sat down, motioning for me to join him. He left his legs open, obviously intending for me to sit there. I hesitated for a moment, uncertain about the close proximity.

"Terrence, I'm not sitting with you like that," I told him with a raised eyebrow.

"Why not? Do you think I'm gonna bite your or something?" He held his arms out toward me, flashing his sexy smile. Shaking my head, I walked over to sit down between his legs, but I misjudged the distance and ended up falling right into his lap.

"That's not what I meant, but this works too," he mumbled into my ear as he wrapped his arms around me. I lightly smacked his arm and looked back at him with a small scowl, wondering how he had gone from sad to horny in the span of less than a minute. The scowl melted away when I saw that there was still pain in his eyes, which he quickly tried to hide by looking away from me.

"I'm sorry," Terrence shook his head. "I don't even know where that came from, my head is-"

"I get it," I interrupted. "You're just trying to think about something else. It's cool." I assured him. He gave me what appeared to be a grateful smile as I moved away from his lap into the empty space in front of him. He kept his arms around me, and I was glad for the contact. I *loved* being close to him.

As the movie progressed, I found myself focused on the defined muscles of his thighs instead of the screen. Because of the way we were seated, his basketball shorts had pulled up on his legs, exposing strong ripples of bare, bronzed flesh. I wasn't considering anything except the magnetism between my fingers and his skin when I reached out to touch him. I tried to be slick about it, pressing my hands down on his legs for leverage to make a subtle shift in position. I left them there, soaking up that feeling until it wasn't enough anymore.

I began tracing figure eights on his thighs with either hand, slowly leading the pattern higher and higher as I leaned back into his body.

What the hell are you doing, Gabi?

My position between his legs helped me gauge his reaction to my touch. I could feel him pressing into me, growing harder, until Terrence gently grabbed my wrists and pulled my hands away from him.

"Gabi, I don't know what you're trying to do, but I'm very close to letting you take advantage of me in my vulnerable state." He was laughing, but there was a strain in his voice.

I clasped a hand over my mouth, mortified by what I'd done. "I wasn't thinking, I'm sorry. I *just* got an attitude with you for the same thing. At least you have an excuse to be a little inappropriate."

"Yeah, that's right. You come in here all touchy-feely while I'm emotional and shit. You're a creep, Gabi," he said, laughing.

"Oh my God....I *am* a creep, aren't I?"

We both burst out laughing. I was incredibly glad that we were able to get past that awkward moment. We talked and laughed through the rest of the movie, and I was happy that I he seemed to be in a much better mood than he had been when I first knocked on the door.

TERRENCE

"Terrence? Terrence! Wake up, bro, you're drooling into your laptop."

I forced my eyes open at the sound of Tarryn's voice in front of my face. She was hovering over me with her hand cupping my chin as she shook my head from side to said.

"Damn, Tarryn, can you stop?"

"Ugh, grumpy-pants. I was just trying to let you know it's getting late, and I know you probably want to get back to your apartment." She placed her hands on her hips as she straightened her posture.

I had gone to the house to wait on her to return from her follow-up appointment with her oncologist. Even though I had a contract deadline that was fast-approaching, I always made sure to be available for Tarryn after any big appointment she had. Instead of lounging around while I waited, I had decided to take work with me, but fatigue had taken over. I fell asleep at the kitchen counter with my head in my laptop.

I ran a hand over the side of my face, frowning at the indentations the buttons from my keyboard had left in my forehead. "Sorry for snapping at you T. How did the appointment go?"

"Cancer free, come back in three months."

"Good!" I said, standing up to pull her into a hug. She squealed when I lifted her from the ground. "Have you told Neil yet?"

"I called him from the car. He's on his way over."

"So are you two officially back together?"

She looked around, making sure we were alone before answering. "He asked me to move in with him."

"Wow, that's...that's big, Tarryn. Are you gonna do it?"

I admired Neil for his persistence with Tarryn. She hadn't made it easy for them to be together. Just like Regina wasn't making it easy for Dorian. Just like Gabi wasn't making it easy for me.

"I don't know." She took a seat at the counter. "Like you said, it's big. Really big. He actually proposed last month, but I told him it was too soon."

"You refused him? That couldn't have gone well." I scratched my jaw, groaning at how that dismissal must have felt. I knew that Neil loved Tarryn, but I also knew that most men, myself included, didn't take rejection well.

"He was mostly cool. He understands that I'm worried about him being stuck with a sick wife. He says that it doesn't matter to him, that he'll support me through whatever, but...I don't know, Terrence. Part of me wants to just let go and enjoy it, but the thought of him wasting away like daddy did...it hurts."

I reached forward to grab her hand. "Tarryn, you can't worry about that. If you spend all of your time worrying about the what-ifs, you're going to end up missing out. Before mama died, she and dad were happy together, for a long time. Don't you want that?"

"I do."

"Then stop being stupid."

"You've got some nerve!" Tarryn said, slapping me on the arm. "The way you run your ass out of here after dinner on Sundays to see Gabi, even though you look at her *all damn day*, every day..."

"That's different."

"No it's not!"

"It really is." I rested my elbow on the counter. "It's...complicated."

"Yeah, yeah, so you've said before. And I still don't buy it. I *know* you like her."

"I do, but she says she wants to keep it friendly, since we work together. I'm gonna respect that," I said, raising my hands in defeat. "What else can I do?"

"Just keep being yourself, Terrence, she'll come around. You gonna wait on her?"

"I don't know that I have a choice."

"Awwwwww!" Tarryn shrieked, covering her mouth with her hands. "You're falling in love with her!"

"No I'm not, Tarryn. Cut that shit out, girl. You and Dorian need to chill."

"Mmmhmm! I can see it all in your face."

———

"Huh?" Gabi asked, finally tearing her gaze away from the window in the my office. "Right about what?"

"I was telling you that you were right about Parker Investments. They settled, just like you said," I replied as she turned her eyes back to the view of the city. I took the opportunity to enjoy the view of *her* in her slim fitting black pants and buttery yellow sweater. When she glanced back, with a smile on her face, I didn't care that she had caught me staring at her. She was beautiful, of course I was staring.

"What's that?" She pointed at something in the darkening sky. I stood from my seat on the edge of the desk and joined her at the window, looking in the direction she indicated.

"*That* is the SkyView in Centennial Park. Is this your first time noticing it? It's been open since July, and it's October now."

"Do you think I wouldn't have mentioned a big ass Ferris wheel in the middle of the city if I'd noticed it before?" She laughed as she continued looking out of the window. "I haven't been that way in a while, and you can't see it from here during the day. Or maybe you can, but it doesn't catch your eye like it does at night. Will you take me?" She grabbed my hands as she turned to me with a grin, her eyes sparkling against the light.

"I...Uh, yeah," I said. I would do anything for her when she was looking at me like that. "You wanna go now?"

"Can we? I *love* stuff like that!"

"Of course we can go now." She was damn near bursting with happiness, shimmying and moving while she waited for me to shut my laptop down. I loved that she was so laid back that even little things like an overpriced Ferris wheel could bring her so much joy.

———

GABI LOOPED her arm through mine as we took our last revolution on the SkyView. She seemed enthralled by the twinkling lights of the city, pointing out different sights for me to see.

"You're like a little kid out here," I said, chuckling as her eyes lit up for what had to be the hundredth time that night.

"I'm sorry. I know it probably seems silly to you, but this makes me really happy. It reminds me of summers with my aunt and uncle, before she died."

"It doesn't seem silly at all," I assured her. I frowned as a drop of liquid appeared on the window of the gondola, quickly followed by several more.

"Oh no!" Gabi said, disappointed as a light, but steady rain began to fall just as our ride ended.

"It's ok. So we'll get a little wet. It probably won't do much more than this drizzle." I started leading her back to car, as quickly as I could, but the light rainfall turned into a downpour well before we reached the car. As soon as we were inside, I cranked up the heat, hoping that it would help us dry out some.

"Can you use your phone and see what the weather is doing?" I asked Gabi as I fastened my seatbelt.

"Already got it pulled up," she said. "It looks like it's about to get pretty nasty." She held the screen in front of me to show me the storm on the radar. "I'm not even sure we should be driving in it."

"Well, we can't stay here, but my place is closer than yours. We'll head there, if that's ok with you?"

"I'm sitting here in soaking wet clothes, Terrence, I will go anywhere you take me as long as it has warm blankets and heat."

"My place it is then."

The trip to my apartment took longer than usual in the low visibility. I pulled Gabi into my room, where I asked her to wait while I retrieved towels from my bathroom. When I stepped out of the bathroom, Gabi was already out of her jacket and boots, and was pulling her damp sweater over her head.

Damn.

She didn't notice me standing there, but I couldn't look away as she tugged the sweater over her hair. When it was off, she peeled away the tank top that she had been wearing with it, appearing to check for dampness. She sucked her teeth, obviously displeased, and then tossed both pieces to the floor. My eyes traveled the soft plane of her stomach, up to her full breasts, covered in a simple black bra.

Damn.

The ends of her hair were wet, and sticking to her golden brown skin. When my gaze made it up to her face, her eyes locked with mine.

"Can I have the towel, Terrence?" She didn't break the stare.

"Yeah." I stepped forward, unfolding one of the towels. When I reached her, I wrapped it around her and pulled her closer to me. She gasped, but didn't pull away.

Gabi lowered her eyes for a moment, as if she were trying to make a decision, and then looked up at me again before she cupped my ears, bringing my lips down to meet hers. At first, I let her set the pace of the kiss, since she initiated it, but I couldn't resist easing my tongue into her mouth, teasing and tasting her. I could feel the blood rush between my legs as she moaned, pressing her body even closer to mine. She stiffened when I slipped my hands underneath the towel, grasping her at the waist.

"Oh, God, Terrence, I'm sorry, I-- I don't know-- why I did that. We... we *can't* do this. I know, I'm sending mixed signals, but I--"

Shit.

"Gabi, come on, don't start crying on me." I wrapped my arms around her neck, pulling her head against my chest as she sobbed. "If you don't stop, I'm gonna start crying too, and that is *not* a sight you wanna see, ok?"

That made her laugh, and a few minutes later, I had her back to her happy self. We changed into dry clothes, in separate rooms. Then we watched TV on my couch until she fell asleep against my chest. I didn't bring it up again, but the fact that *she* had kissed me was definitely not forgotten.

GABI

A few weeks after I kissed Terrence, I was sitting in my parent's dining room in Chicago. It seemed like only the family members I didn't know or couldn't stand had shown up to dinner this year. I picked at the plate in front of me, which my mother had insisted on preparing. While the rest of the table feasted on the usual Christmas meal, she had decided I only needed green beans, collards, and carrots. She had noticed the weight I'd gained, even though I had shed all but the last five pounds through my hard work with Terrence. But I wasn't going to bother explaining that to her. I excused myself from the table and headed into the living room, where I hadn't been seated a full minute before the doorbell rang.

Looking through the peephole, I rolled my eyes at Michael's grinning face. I started not to answer, but I knew that one of my parents would if I didn't. I wasn't interested in starting any more drama, so I opened the door.

"What, Michael?" I asked, with a scowl on my face.

"Merry Christmas, Gabi." He raked his eyes over my body, settling his stare on my breasts. "No mistletoe over the door?"

I crossed my arms over my chest to block his view. "What do you want?"

"You know what I want, Gabi, but I'm not here for that," he said with a smirk. "Your parents invited me to Christmas dinner."

"You're late."

"Because I just finished my shift at the hospital. They said I could stop by any time."

I stepped back, allowing him into the foyer. "I bet they did."

"So...you're looking well enough."

"Kiss my ass Mike."

"You've certainly got plenty of it now. I guess lawyers have a "freshman fifteen" too, huh?" he asked, laughing at this own joke.

"I'm 5'8", and weigh 162 pounds. That's *hardly* worthy of fat jokes, asshole."

"Watch that mouth of yours, young lady," my father said as he stepped into the foyer. He glared at me as he reached out to shake Michael's hand. "Thanks for joining us, son. I'm sure Gabi would like to fix you a plate." He sent a pointed look in my direction.

"I'll pass." I narrowed my eyes and gave my father a tight, forced smile. "Michael is an adult, I'm sure he can feed himself."

"You need the practice, sweetheart," he replied, clenching his jaw.

"What could fixing a plate possibly prepare me for, Father?"

"Becoming Michael's wife." He crossed his arms as he stared at me, waiting on my response.

"That's never gonna happen."

"Is it because of Terrence Whitaker?" Michael stepped forward, so that he was right beside my father. I wanted nothing more than to slap the nasty little smirk off of his face.

"Who the hell is Terrence Whitaker?" My father asked angrily.

"Some second-rate, sob story lawyer with no parents. He works at the firm with Gabi, and she's been spending a *lot* of time with him. Too much."

I clenched my jaw, narrowing my eyes at Michael as he spoke. How did he know *any* information about what I was doing in Atlanta?

"Are you *stalking* me?" I walked right up to Michael's face, my lip twitching in rage. His ugly smirk faltered, but a second later he was back in step.

"I hope you don't think you can replace me with him. He'll never be the kind of man I am, never be as successful as me, never as much money as me. He'll never be *me*."

"That would be the whole point, Michael. You see, I'm not the same little 17 year old girl that was *so* proud to have a man who was 20 years old and in college. I see you for what you really are, and I don't want anything to do with it." I crossed my arms over my chest, staring defiantly into his face. If he wanted a fight, he could definitely get it.

"So it's true, Gabrielle? You've been running around with another man?" my father asked, scowling.

"I was assigned to him," I explained. "I'm basically his legal assistant for the year. When he and I are together, we're usually working. But, I don't even know why I'm explaining this, *I'm grown!* And aside from that, I'm also single, so I don't see why it would be a problem if I *was* "running around" with him."

"What the hell has gotten into you? Are you *trying* to shame this family? We have given you everything you could possibly want, and even lined up a husband and a future for you. Is this blatant disrespect what we get in return for that?"

"It's *not* disrespectful to want to live my own life. You don't want respect, you want obedience!"

"How can you stand here and say such a thing, Gabrielle?" my mother's dramatic words made me turn to face her. "Why are you trying to ruin Christmas, little girl?"

These folks are insane. That's the only explanation.

She pressed her hands against her temples as if I were giving her a headache. "First you show up in our home four sizes bigger than you left, and now here you are, disrespecting poor Michael and your father."

Am I in the twilight zone?

"Ruining Christmas? *Seriously?* Wow. I just…I'm gonna go sit in my room, so I don't screw up anything else."

I shoved past Michael to get up the stairs, ignoring any comments that were tossed my way. Once I was in my room, I immediately closed and locked the door, flopping down on the bed with my tablet. I was relieved to see that there were still flights going out on Christmas day. I rescheduled my return to Atlanta on the first available plane, paying the $100 adjustment fee without hesitation. Then, I called a cab, and began stuffing the few things I had unpacked back into my suitcase. I watched the street in front of the house until I saw the cab pull up, then grabbed my bags, thankful that I had packed lightly enough to only need two. I left the expensive luxury gifts from my parents in their wrappings on the bed.

Peeking my head down the stairs, I made sure the foyer was empty before I dashed down with my bags, stopping to put on my outerwear before I stepped outside into the wind and cold. I shoved my bag into the trunk of the cab and directed the driver to take me to the airport. Just 30 minutes after I had been accused of ruining Christmas, I was headed back home, to Atlanta.

———

"MERRY CHRISTMAS, GABI. " -T. Whitaker

"Merry Christmas to you too Terrence."

"Are you having a good time with your famiyl?" -T. Whitaker

"*family, I mean."-T. Whitaker

"I knew what you meant, lol, you didn't have to correct that. I'm actually having a better time now that I'm NOT with my family any more."

"What do you mean? Why aren't you with your family?" -T. Whitaker

"I left early. At the airport."

"What happened?" -T. Whitaker

"They suck, that's what happened."

"Elaborate." -T. Whitaker

"They said I ruined dinner because I'm fat and won't marry Michael."

"Wow. That's....interesting. So you're spending Christmas alone, at the airport?" -T. Whitaker

"You make it sound really pathetic!"

"Well...." -T. Whitaker

"Oh, shut up."

"When is your flight?" -T. Whitaker

"Soon. We're about to start boarding in a few minutes."

"How long is the flight?" -T. Whitaker

"Like 2 hours. Not too long."

"I'll come pick you up. Call me when you land." -T. Whitaker

"No. You should enjoy yourself with your great family. I'll get a cab."

"I'm leaving soon anyway. Tarryn is about to go meet up with Neil, and my Aunt and her lil boyfriend are hinting around that they want to be alone." -T. Whitaker

"LMBO! They nasty."

"Don't say that shit Gabi, I don't wanna think about that." -T. Whitaker

"Do you think he calls her Peaches?"

"Please, Gabi." -T. Whitaker

"I'll let you know when I'm back in Atlanta."

"Call me, when your plane lands." -T. Whitaker

———

I HEADED to the bag carousel to pick up my luggage. The quicker I had my bags, the sooner I could hail a cab to take me back to my apartment. There was no way I was pulling Terrence away from his family on Christmas. I would call him when I was back in my apartment. He had rescued me so many times I was afraid he was going to start seeing me as helpless. I didn't want to be that girl. For nearly 6 years of our 8 year relationship, I had leaned on Michael for everything. Then, at 23, something clicked.

He was taking full advantage of the fact that I turned to him for even the littlest things, trying to make me feel like I couldn't do anything without him. If I tried to make a friend, he acted like I was abandoning him, so I stopped trying. Back then, I was so focused on him and school that I didn't miss those relationships, but thinking back on it, I hated him for that. Regina had great friends from college, women that she could call for anything. I didn't have that, because I let him convince me that I didn't need it.

I started reading books on relationships and boundaries, and I quickly realized just how dysfunctional our relationship really was. I thanked God for that clarity. When I started pushing back against his efforts to control me, our relationship completely changed. For about a year, I had hope that we could actually make it work. Until I learned about the countless women, and Michael's penchant for risky sexual behavior. The next year, we were done, and I made a vow that I wouldn't be vulnerable like that with anyone.

Then, Terrence came along, and my heart drop-kicked my common sense off the side of Stone Mountain.

I spotted one of my bags and reached for it, but I wasn't fast enough to keep someone from grabbing the handle.

What the hell?

My breath caught in my throat as Terrence easily lifted my bags from the carousel. "I'll take that."

He came for me!

"How did you know that was mine?" I asked, crossing my arms to feign annoyance, even though I was fighting to keep a grin off of my face.

"Gabi, how could these bags *not* be yours?" He gave a pointed look to the coral and grey luggage before turning back to me.

"Am I that obvious?

He laughed, a sound that I didn't realize I missed until that moment. "Yes, you absolutely are. You ready to go home?"

"I am beyond ready to get home, take the hottest shower I can stand, and veg out in front of the TV with some hot cocoa."

"Want some company?"

My head shot up as I turned to him, wide-eyed. Did he mean...

"For the TV and hot cocoa, Gabi. Get your mind out of the gutter, damn!"

I playfully punched him in the arm. "Whatever! Yes, I would like some company, if you don't have anything else to do."

"There's nowhere else I'd rather be."

TERRENCE

*D*amn, that smells good.

I dragged my eyes open to see Gabi sitting on the floor in front of me, holding a steaming mug of hot cocoa under my nose. After bringing her to her apartment, I decided to watch TV while she showered, but my body apparently had other plans, and I had fallen asleep stretched out on the couch.

"Wake up, sleepyhead."

She smiled, then placed the mug on the coffee table and leaned back on her hands while I moved into a seated position.

"Why are you sitting on the floor?"

"I was about to rub on your beard while you were sleeping, but I realized just how creepy that was once I was down here. It's comfortable down here though."

She pulled her knees up to her chest and wrapped her arms around them, giving me a mostly unobstructed view of the smooth backs of her thighs. I averted my eyes back to her face, trying to push the picture from my mind, but it was too late.

"Come sit up on the couch with me, silly girl," I said, hoping that my thoughts would become less inappropriate if she were beside me.

It got worse. She used my outstretched hand for balance as she stood up, unintentionally sexy in a tee shirt and pajama shorts. Once she was on her feet, she held an envelope in front of me, then dropped it into my hands as she sat down, so close that our legs were touching.

"What is this?"

"Your Christmas gift!" She smiled, her eyes sparkling with excitement. "Open it!"

"You think I don't know you keep a box of generic Christmas cards around for when you forget to get gifts for people?"

"Shut up and open it, fool."

I broke the seal on the envelope and pulled out the card.

"It's a year supply of protein powder that actually tastes good," Gabi blurted out, before I could even open the card. "That stuff you were drinking after your workouts was disgusting, so I researched and taste tested until I found one that was good, and *actually* has a better nutrient breakdown than the one you were using. You'll get a delivery every month."

Wow.

"This... this is pretty damn cool, Gabi."

"I know," she said, grinning as she popped an imaginary collar.

"You're so damn cocky." I laughed as I pulled her into a hug, planting a quick kiss on her forehead. "Thank you."

"You're welcome! So..."

"You're wondering if I got you something?"

"Bingo!"

For a moment, I considered pretending that I hadn't, but the thought of taking that smile off her face put a sour taste in my mouth. I took a sip from my now room-temperature cocoa and pointed to the envelope I'd placed on the coffee table while she was in the shower.

"You didn't even notice it, did you?"

"I didn't!" She leaned forward to snatch it up, biting down on her bottom lip as she carefully opened it. A confused look crossed her face as she opened the card, then unfolded the letter that was included within. I knew the exact moment when she had read the post-script, because her hand flew up to cover her mouth. She looked up at me with tears in her eyes, swallowing several times before she spoke.

"Ellen Atkins is my *idol*, Terrence." She shook her head, looking down at the letter in awe. "She is one of the best black lawyers in the country, and she wrote to *me*. This isn't just some shitty generic letter either! She says she read the article I wrote about her, and that she looked me up. She looked *me* up!

Listen to this: '*I know that in your article, you mention several times that you consider me your hero. No, Gabrielle. You, and other young women like you, are MY heroes. Seeing a smart, motivated, beautiful, (as Mr. Whitaker insisted on reminding me!) young woman becoming a lawyer lets me know that the hardships that I faced as a new lawyer, fighting for recognition and workplace equality were more than worth it. I am honored to have been able to pave the way for you.*'"

She stopped reading to look up at me again. "Terrence, how could you possibly know to do this? *How* did you do this?"

"I read your article too," I said. "It was in your file, so I read it, and I could just feel how much admiration and respect you had for her. I looked her up, and found out that she lived in Dallas. So, when I had to take that trip there with Mr. Pritchard to meet a client, I got in contact with her, and I told her all about you. The next day, she asked me to come by office, so I did, and she gave me that letter to give to you. And she told me to tell you that she wants to meet you. So," I reached into her lap to hold up the other item in the card, which she hadn't noticed, "this is an airline voucher, so that whenever you get a chance, you can go meet your 'she-ro', as my mom used to say."

"This is *amazing*, Terrence. I don't even really know what to say!"

"Say you're gonna go within a year, before that voucher expires. That thing is non-refundable."

Gabi laughed as she slapped my leg. She gave the letter another long look before she brought her eyes back up to my face. "Thank you. This really means a lo-- wait a minute... when you went to Dallas, we were mad at each other! It was during that whole Josh thing. So you did this for me anyway, even though you were upset with me?"

I shrugged, dropping my eyes down to the heavy slip of paper that was still in my hand. "Yeah, I was upset, but that didn't change the fact that I care about you. Even if we had never recovered from that... I knew it would mean a lot to you, so I did what I had to do to make it happen, hurt feelings aside."

Gabi didn't reply. Instead, she placed a hand against the side of my face and leaned in to place a kiss on my cheek. She lingered there for a moment before she moved, pressing her cocoa-sweetened lips into mine. It was a barely there kiss, as if she were unsure about the decision to do it. I gave back a little pressure of my own, hoping that she would let go of whatever was holding her back. She responded my teasing the seam of my lips with her tongue, and I welcomed it, because I wanted more. I wanted *her*.

At first, our kisses were soft, and slow. Gentle, tentative kisses to gauge reactions. But with each touch, they became less about want, and more about need. I *needed* my hands against the soft flesh of her waist, needed my mouth and tongue against her lips, then her chin, then her neck. It wasn't until she spoke that I realized that at some point, she had pushed her way into my lap, and was straddling my legs.

"Terrence..."

"Yeah?"

"You wanna go to my room?"

"What's wrong with right here?"

"My roommate, Terrence. We can't do this here."

I ran my hands up her thighs, cupping her butt with both hands before I stood. She yelped, but wrapped her legs around my waist as I carried her, following the directions to her room between kisses.

As soon as the door closed behind us, her hands were at my belt, unbuckling it so that my jeans could drop to the floor. Then, on the hem of my shirt, which I helped her tug over my head. I pulled her over to the bed, where I sat down, positioned her between my legs, and then began removing her clothes.

"Wait a minute." She stopped my hands as they pulled up on her shirt. "Let me unplug that," she said, pointing to the scented plug-in beside the bed, which had a dim light, the only light, throughout the room.

"For what?" I held her at the waist, not wanting her to move. I knew exactly why she wanted the light off, and I didn't like it.

"Because I would feel more comfortable if it wasn't on."

"Why?"

She rolled her eyes, obviously annoyed that I was pushing the issue. "Because, my body isn't... It's not what it was when I first came to Atlanta eight months ago."

"But you've been working hard at the gym."

"Yeah, but my stomach... it still needs work."

I tugged at the front of her shirt, forcing her to take a

step forward. "Do you really think I give a shit about that, Gabi? I think your body is perfect."

She scoffed at that, pushing me away. "Yeah right, Terrence. Why are you at the gym with me twice a week then?"

"Because you want me to be. You mentioned that you were unhappy with your body, and you accepted my offer for help because you wanted to change it. That has nothing to do with *my* perception of you."

"So you don't see any flaws when you look at me?" she asked, crossing her arms over her chest.

"I didn't say that. Everybody has flaws. I said I thought you were perfect. There's a difference." I pulled her arms away from her chest, and then reached up to cup her face in my hands. "Do you understand what I'm trying to say to you?"

Gabi was quiet for a moment, then gave a barely perceptible nod of her head before she spoke. "I think so."

"Good. Now stop playing, and let me see you."

She smiled, and I leaned back on my elbows as I watched her slowly strip away her clothes. When she was done, she wouldn't meet my eyes. She was shifting her weight nervously between her feet, and her fingers were twitching as if she wanted nothing more than to cover herself up.

"Beautiful," I said, sitting up so that I could press my lips into the soft flesh near her belly button. I let my hands and eyes roam, exploring her body as I kissed every place I could reach. "Gabi, you are one interesting girl." I grinned as I ran my fingers over a tiny tattoo of the justice scales, located just above her rib cage.

"That little thing hurt like crazy too." She laughed, fully relaxing into my touch. The sound sent a surprising amount of warmth through my body, and I realized just how happy I was to with her, and it had nothing to do with her current state of nudity. Her skin was like velvet, warm and silky to the touch. I didn't want to take my hands off of her. I *couldn't* take my hands off of her.

"Come here." I pulled her into my lap, and began trailing kisses over her neck. She moaned when I cupped her breasts in my hands, dragging my fingers over her nipples until they peaked under my touch. Her moans turned into a gasp when I lowered my head to cover them with my mouth. She was gripping the back of my head, holding me in place, and when I slid my fingers inside of her, she dug her fingers into my shoulders, rolling her hips in response.

"Terrence, this isn't enough... I need to feel you." Gabi had her hands at the waistband of my boxers, trying to pull them down even though I was seated. I chuckled at her, then lifted myself so that she could remove them. She didn't waste any time lowering herself onto me, surrounding me in her wetness and warmth.

Damn, she feels good.

I grabbed her thighs, stopping her before she could begin grinding her hips against me.

"Don't move," I groaned into her ear as I tried to calm my body's reaction.

"What's wrong?" She was moving anyway, gripping her pelvic muscles around me.

"Shit, Gabi, it's been a *while*, and I am trying my hardest not disappoint you, but..." We locked eyes for a moment, and then, as if we were thinking the same thing, burst out laughing. It was a full minute before either of us regained our composure. I wrapped my arms around her, pulling her close so that my face was resting between her breasts.

When I looked up, Gabi was grinning down at me, rubbing her hands across my shoulders. "I'm sorry, I didn't mean to laugh, but your face..." She dipped her face toward mine for a kiss.

"You hurt my feelings," I teased, sucking her bottom lip into my mouth, then gently biting down on it. She whimpered into my mouth, then ground her hips into mine.

"Please say you're ready now." The laughter was gone. She sounded desperate now.

"Go for it baby." The words were barely out of my mouth before she began moving against me, in a pace that started out sensual and slow, but gradually became frenzied as she began losing control. She was *so* wet, and *so* tight, and she felt *so damn good*. I gripped her thighs, gently guiding her into a slower pace that made both of us sweat from the prolonged gratification.

"Terrence, please, I need to go faster."

I released my hold, letting her create her own rhythm, which soon had her legs shaking.

"I need more... deeper." She moaned that demand right into my ear, and that, plus the sight of her breasts bobbing up and down and she ground her hips into me made me even harder than I already was. I gently bit down into the soft flesh of her neck as I gripped her waist, meeting her downward thrusts with upward strokes of my own.

"Terrence, deeper."

"I don't wanna hurt you..."

"Damn it, just do it."

I flipped us over, positioning myself between her legs before I began stroking again. She locked her legs around my waist as I drove into her. I leaned forward to kiss her throat, and she wrapped her arms around my neck, keeping me close to her. Her eyes were closed, and she was biting down on her lip in pleasure.

"Mmmmmm."

I moved into long, slow strokes as her eyes fluttered open. My eyes nearly rolled back in my head at the sight of her raising her own hands to her nipples, squeezing and pulling them between her fingers as she squirmed underneath me. Then, she was arching her back away from the bed, moaning my name into my ear as she reached her climax. She contracted around me, vaulting me over the edge with her.

We collapsed back onto the bed, both sweating and panting. After we had both cooled off, I pulled her into my arms. Gabi rested her head against my chest, and I kissed the top of her head, burying my fingers in her hair.

"Thank you," she said, looking up at me. She ran her fingers along my eyebrows, then down to my beard, where she absently slid her fingers back and forth..

"For what?"

"Well, for coming to pick me up today, and for the wonderful gift. And... for making me feel beautiful."

"Just *feel* beautiful? Girl you *are* beautiful. Hey, you're not gonna forget my number now, right? You know how women do, get the draws then act like they don't know you anymore."

"Whatever Terrence," Gabi laughed, resting her hand against my face. "No, I'm not gonna treat you like a stranger. But, we should probably still keep things cool around the office."

"That's probably wise." I thought back to the conversation I'd had with Mr. Graham about Gabi. We'd had many other conversations since then, and she was actually a frequent subject, but it was always about her performance. There was never a repeat of the warning he'd given me that first day. I wondered how he would react when he found out just how involved I was.

GABI

What the hell is weighing me down?

I slowly opened my eyes, taking in the bright morning sun shining into my bedroom. As the synapses in my brain began to fire, further waking me, I realized that Terrence had his arm wrapped around my waist, and that my butt was very firmly nestled into an impressive morning erection. More clarity flooded in, and my brain rudely informed me that I was nude. I was spooning with Terrence, and I was nude.

Terrence had touched and kissed places I didn't even know existed. I grinned as I remembered him waking me up several times that night to make love again.

Surprisingly, I didn't feel at all embarrassed about that thought. Even though we were together for years, I always felt a slight sense of shame after being with Michael. When we finished, or, more accurately, when *he* finished, he would immediately roll away from me. There was never any cuddling, he was in too big of a hurry to wash up and leave, so that he could go "study" or start his shift at the hospital. I was almost relieved when I found out that he was cheating, because it gave me an excuse to stop sleeping with him, so I could stop feeling cheap and used.

Laying here with Terrence couldn't be a more different experience. He was awake now, kissing the bare skin of shoulders as he attempted to pull me even closer. I didn't feel taken advantage of at all. I felt *wanted*, and it was incredible.

"Good morning beautiful," he mumbled, burying his face into my hair.

"Good morning to you too." I gasped as he slid his hand between my thighs, lifting my leg up in what I assumed was an attempt to start round...four, maybe? "Whoa, Terrence," I stopped him, clamping my legs shut.

"What's wrong? Are you sore?"

"That's not why I stopped you," I said, turning to face him. "I know we got a little carried away last night, but don't you think we should at least *try* to use some protection?"

"That's not a problem, beautiful," he said. "I'll run to the store, but I wanna show you something first." He slipped out of the bed, stopping to pull on his boxers before he reached into his jeans for his phone. Climbing back into the bed beside me, he made a few gestures on the screen before handing it to me.

"What is this?" I asked as I took it, thumbing across the screen. I took me a moment to realize I was looking at the same type of documents I had started getting religiously after I learned of Michael's inability to be monogamous. STD testing results. More importantly, *negative* test results, from just a month before.

"I scan a copy of all my important documents and store them online. I'm glad I do, because I wanted you to see this. Just for the record," Terrence said, slipping his arms around my waist, "I don't make unprotected sex a habit, and I get tested regularly, even it's been a while. Last night, we were just kind of wrapped up in the moment. I wouldn't put your health at risk, Gabi."

"Thank you for showing me this, but diseases aren't the *only* concern."

"What, you mean a baby? My aunt and sister would be thrilled about that."

"I'm not about to have any babies, are you crazy?" I asked, turning my head to scowl at him. "You're getting way ahead of yourself Mr. Whitaker."

"I'm just playing with you Gabi."

"Yeah, you'd better be. Lucky for you, my *hilarious* room-mate stuffed a box of condoms into my hand the day I moved in, so you don't have to go to the store," I said, reaching into the nightstand drawer for a handful of condoms.

"So why are we still talking, instead of doing?"

"That's an excellent question."

———

"I STILL CAN'T BELIEVE you're actually working the day after Christmas. This is kind of obsessive, Terrence."

"You have a tattoo of justice scales, and *I'm* obsessed?" Terrence shook his head as he stood from his chair at the office. "You enjoy doing contracts and you know it."

"I do, but I can think of quite a few things I would enjoy more," I said, pulling at the waistband of his jeans.

"We can get to that, I just need to leave this on Mr. Graham's desk."

I followed him down the hall, and when we reached Uncle Bobby's office, I opened the door, assuming he was still in Florida visiting what I considered the "good" side of our family, meaning the non-stuck-up ones. For a second, I wished I had accepted the invitation to join him, but then I wouldn't have ended up spending Christmas with Terrence.

When I realized that Terrence hadn't moved, I looked into the office, wondering what had him standing in the doorway frozen.

I had assumed wrong. Very, very, *very* wrong. The receptionist, Vanessa, was on Uncle Bobby's desk with her legs in the air and her head thrown back. And my wonderful uncle was sitting in his desk chair in front of her, with his head buried between her thighs. I felt my stomach clench up, and just as I was about to let out a startled shriek, Terrence clamped his hand over my mouth and dragged me back, carefully closing the door behind us.

"*Oh my God!* Oh my God! Did that really just happen?" I squealed as soon as we were back in Terrence's office.

"It definitely happened. I never would have guessed Mr. Graham was a freak! On his desk, of all places!"

I flopped down in a chair, trying to erase the image from my brain. "Ohhh, please just make it stop! I could have gone my entire life and not seen my Uncle Bobby like that!"

"... Gabi, who?"

"Mr. Graham, my Uncle Bo--... oh, shit."

Terrence sat down in the empty seat beside me, with a grim expression on his handsome face. "Did you just tell me that Robert Graham is your *uncle*, Gabi?"

"Umm... yes?"

"Gabi, why wouldn't you tell me something like that?"

"Because, I didn't want anybody thinking it was the only reason I got a position here. I couldn't tell anyone from the office, Regina is the only person who knew." I reached forward, attempting to place a hand on his knee, but he moved away. There was agitation etched into his narrowed eyes and clenched jaw.

"So you're telling me that I almost lost my job for you over a mistake, when you wouldn't have even gotten in trouble for it anyway?"

"Terrence, no! He wouldn't have shown me any favoritism, he would have reprimanded me the same as he would anyone else!"

"Gabi, he's your uncle. You're his family. Is *that* why he hinted that I needed to stay away from you? So you could be available for your ex?" His voice was raised now. Not yelling, but enough that I knew he was really upset.

"I had no idea he even said anything like that to you about me!"

He sucked his teeth, cocking an eyebrow at me.

"Yeah, right. What was last night, some type of rebellion against your family? This entire time you've been talking about keeping things professional, but your family makes you mad on Christmas, and all of a sudden you're not worried about that anymore. I know they want you with this Michael guy. What am I, your way to piss them off?"

Tears sprang to my eyes as I took in his words.

Does he really believe this?!

"Terrence, *no*. I wouldn't do something like that!"

"Well that's exactly what it looks like Gabi, when you're keeping shit from me. You can't tell me that after all the time we've spent getting to know each other, you think that *I* would have seen you differently if I knew that Mr. Graham was your uncle. I know how smart you are. You were more than qualified for your position," he said, standing up and walking towards the door. "You had to know that if I was seen as an obstacle for your family, he would have no issue eliminating the problem. Did you think I wouldn't pursue you if I knew?"

"It's not just that, it's..." I trailed off, remembering that I still couldn't tell the whole story. Uncle Bobby had forbidden me from mentioning Terrence's promotion to him, which was the reason why I hadn't revealed my little secret. He was reacting just as badly as I thought he would. Even if I *could* tell him, I'm not sure he would take very kindly to my unintentional part in the deception.

"It's what?"

"I *can't* tell you. I wish I could, but I--"

"So you're still gonna hold something else back?"

I knew I probably looked a mess with my face streaked with tears, but I didn't care. Yes, I lied, but it wasn't for the hurtful reason he was thinking. "*Terrence*, please, just let me exp-"

"I can't do this right now, Gabi. I thought that after last night, things had changed between us, but apparently not. I'll see you Monday when the office officially opens."

Before I could say another word, he was out the door. I guess he had forgotten that *he* drove.

----*Terrence*----

"YOU LEFT *her at the office*? Are you crazy? You know what, don't answer that. You *have* to be crazy."

Tarryn scowled at me from across the table, shaking her head. I'd already reminded her several times that we were supposed to be having a good time, not rehashing my drama with Gabi, but she wouldn't leave it alone. We were celebrating her birthday a week early, because Neil was taking her on a vacation somewhere tropical for the actual day. I hoped that getting out, relaxing, and having a few drinks with my sister would give me a chance to clear my head, but that obviously wasn't in her plans.

"I didn't actually leave. Once I got to my car, I remembered that she rode with me. I went back up to get her, tried to call her, no response. When I couldn't find her in the office, I finally left. I went by her place but nobody answered, so I decided to just leave her alone."

"You messed up bad, baby bro."

"I messed up? Gabi is the one who lied!" I slouched back in my seat, glad that she had chosen a booth for the night.

"Terrence... stop it. You know damn well why she didn't tell anybody that her uncle was the boss. She didn't want people thinking she was some spoiled little girl who was getting by on her family's name. It's understandable."

"No it's not. She could have told *me*."

"Terrence, by the time y'all got close like that, it was probably just second nature for her to refer to him as boss man to you. She really didn't do anything wrong, and you need to come off of your high horse about it. I mean, you don't really believe that 'using you to rebel against her family' bullshit that you told me, do you?" She cocked an eyebrow at me, waiting for a response.

"Once I had the chance to actually think about it... no, not really," I admitted. In that moment of anger, all I saw was betrayal, but looking back at Gabi's *actions*, I knew that I had overreacted. "Tarryn, I don't know what the fuck I'm doing. You know I've never been serious about anybody like this."

Tarryn reached across the table to grab my hand, giving it a light squeeze. "I get that, T. But... Ok, let me say this; you've brought Gabi around enough times that I can read her pretty well. Laid back, happy, she's just a genuinely sweet person, and she loves you, Terrence. And whether or not you're gonna admit it, you love her too. I watched it happen over these last eight months, even though y'all were being stupid. Hell, everybody sees it except y'all! Now, don't get me wrong, I'm definitely not trying to tell you the lie that just love is enough to sustain a relationship, but it's definitely a start."

"Yeah, but... how do I know if it will even work between us?"

Tarryn's fork slipped out of her hand, dropping to the table with a loud clatter. "Uh, Terrence... I don't know if you realize this, but y'all have been basically dating for the last 3 months anyway. The only difference is that now y'all are fuc-- I mean, *making love*."

She pretended to gag into her hand, then shot me a smile from across the table. "Listen, just stop over thinking it. Y'all have enough degrees, diplomas, and common sense to do the best you can. If it works out, that's beautiful. If it doesn't, that's ok too, it's part of life. But you can't be so paralyzed trying to figure out what to do that you don't *do* anything!"

"But--"

"Nope! But nothing. Right now, tell me what you think you need to do."

"I need to apologize." There was no hesitation about my answer to that. I could only imagine how frustrating and hurtful that entire conversation at the office must have been for Gabi. Keeping that secret had to be hard, and my accusation that she was using me couldn't have been any easier for her to swallow. I ran a hand over my face, trying to shake the image of her sitting in my office crying. I *hated* seeing her cry, and I hated being the one responsible for her tears. Just the thought was giving me a headache.

"You're absolutely right, you *do* need to apologize," Tarryn said.

"But she won't even answer my calls."

"She will. She just needs time. Gabi is probably in her apartment, crying into a jar of Talenti... or not."

I followed Tarryn's gaze to see Gabi being led to a table by the hostess. She was immediately followed by an older couple who I assumed were her parents. All similar golden-brown complexions, dark hair, tall, deep-set eyes. She and her mother were nearly mirror images of each other, except her mother's hair was styled into a straight bob that fell just to her chin.

From our booth, I had a perfect vantage point of their table. We were right against the divider, so we could see them, but they couldn't see us. It struck me immediately that Gabi looked like this restaurant was the absolute last place she wanted to be. I had never seen her usually bright, happy eyes look so lifeless.

Neither Tarryn nor I spoke, meals completely forgotten as we watched the tense exchange that started as soon as their waiter stepped away from the table. Gabi's father said something to her, and instead of responding, she crossed her arms over her chest and continued staring at some point on the wall. Her mother made a comment. Still, no response. Finally, her father leaned forward, snatching one of Gabi's arms down from her chest as he whispered angrily into her face. That got a reaction. She snatched away and said something back, her nostrils flared as she spoke. They simply stared at each other for a long, anxious moment before Gabi dragged her eyes away, then placed her arms back over her chest.

Things were calm for several minutes, until the hostess returned to their table, bringing along a man who I recognized as Michael, Gabi's ex. That's when sweet, mild-mannered Gabi lost it. She was out of her seat, and she was speaking, but I couldn't hear what was being said, so I knew she wasn't yelling. I wanted to intervene, but Tarryn warned me to stay in my seat.

"She's gotta work this out for herself Terrence. She's grown."

So I stayed where I was, perched on the edge of the bench, ready to jump up and go to her rescue if things got out of hand. And then, things got out of hand. First, Michael walked up, placing his hands roughly on her shoulders to push her back into her seat. She shoved him away, then gave him the swiftest open-handed slap to the face I'd ever seen, so hard that it actually rocked him on his feet.

"I told you not to ever put your damn hands on me again!"

The entire restaurant went quiet except for the steady clinging of pans in the kitchen, and I could feel the collective intake of breath as we all wondered what was going to happen next.

"*How dare you* embarrass us like this?" Her father was on his feet now, rage clearly imprinted on his face. "You will apologize *now*, to all of these people."

Gabi scoffed, not bothering to hide the disgust on her face. "I will do no such thing. *I* didn't cause this."

"Now, Gabrielle. I will not tell you again."

She crossed her arms over her chest again, her eyes bristling in defiance as she clamped her mouth closed. It seemed like time slowed down as her father drew his hand back, then brought it across Gabi's face with such force that it knocked her to the floor.

I'm going to kill this motherfucker.

"What the-- Tarryn, what the hell are you doing, get off of me!" I hadn't made it two steps out of the booth before Tarryn had grabbed me by the back of my waistband, pulling as hard as she could to keep me in place.

"Terrence, no! You're gonna get yourself arrested, *dummy*, for beating up an old man in a public place. Let security handle it."

"Let go of me, or you're coming too, if I have to drag your ass along!"

"Then get to dragging, baby bro, because I'm not letting you do this. Security can handle it!" she said again, true to her word about not letting go.

I didn't care, not even a little, about getting arrested. All I cared about was the fact that someone who called himself a man, her *father*, had hurt Gabi, and I was going to kick his ass for it. But by the time I made it around the divider, dragging Tarryn along with me, Gabi, Michael, and her parents were all gone.

———

I DROPPED Tarryn off at home, then immediately headed for Gabi's apartment. I had already tried calling at least ten times, but it wouldn't even ring. Everything went straight to voicemail. By the time I made it to her building, I had tried five more times with the same results.

I parked the car, and then headed to her door. I could hear the sounds of Beyonce drifting from inside, and I knew that was Gabi. I knocked once, and after receiving no response, I knocked again, a little louder.

"Gabi, it's Terrence! Please open the door." I waited, hoping that she would answer. I was starting to feel anxious, and I needed to know that she was ok. Just as I was about to raise my hand to knock again, the door opened. We stood there, staring at each other in silence. Her right cheek was bruised, and slightly swollen, and her eyes were filled with a sadness that she tried to hide by dropping her gaze down to her bare toes.

"I...I saw what happened at the restaurant," I said, shoving my hands into the front pockets of my jeans. "I was there with Tarryn. I tried to get to you, but... you were gone too fast."

She pulled her eyes back up to mine. After several more seconds of silence, Gabi swung the door open a little wider and stepped aside, welcoming me in. She stayed beside the now closed door with her top lip pulled into her mouth, biting down on it so hard it seemed like she might draw blood.

I took a step toward her, just intending to distract her, but when she looked up, there were tears in her eyes. I instinctively pulled her into my arms, cupping her head against my chest as she cried. Several moments passed before she stopped, and the only sounds in the room were her quiet sniffles as I led her to the couch to sit down.

"Terrence... I'm sorry for not telling you about Uncle Bobby. If I'd known that-"

"Hey," I interrupted her. "I'm not even tripping about that right now. At all, actually. I'm more concerned with what I saw between you and your parents."

She sighed heavily, picking at the slightly frayed hem of her shorts with her fingernails. I hadn't noticed before, but she was in shorts and a tank top, and her hair was damp.

"Did I interrupt your bedtime routine?" I asked, glancing up at the clock. 9:17 PM.

"Kind of, but it's fine. I usually wouldn't even be getting in the bed this early, but I was honestly hoping that if I went to sleep this would all just go away." She finally succeeded at pulling her hem loose. I watched as she spread it flat against her bare leg and began picking out loose threads.

She pulled her hands into fists. "You know, it's only been since I moved to Atlanta that I realized that they just want to control me. This guy, Michael, that they want me to be with so bad is *awful*. He cheated on me, he disrespected me, and he's tried to get physical with me more than once. You know what my mom said when I told her? 'That comes with the territory of dating and marrying a successful man'. Can you believe that?"

I just nodded as she went on. "You would think that as parents, they would want what's healthy for me. But no. Michael is from a good family, and he's gonna be a doctor. Who cares if he tries to kick my ass every once in a while, right? What kind of parent thinks that?

When I told them I was moving, you would think I'd announced that I was moving to a third world country to be a prostitute, the way they reacted. I thought they were concerned about me getting a job, about my safety, about me being alone. But no. I realize now that they were upset that I was acting outside of their control. They didn't want a thinking, feeling, strong daughter at all. They wanted a puppet. So many of the things they did that I thought were normal... they weren't. And I just..."

Her voice broke as tears began spilling down her face again. I hated that I had no idea what to say to make it better, so I remained silent, but pulled her into my arms again.

A while passed before she lifted her head from my chest, looking up at me with red rimmed eyes. "I've got your shirt soaking wet, I'm sorry."

"Don't sweat it. I already knew you were a crybaby," I said, teasing her. She responded with the first smile I'd seen from her since before my blow up at the office. It was a welcome change. She shifted her body closer to me, then looked up, locking her eyes with mine.

I dipped my head forward, kissing the top of her forehead. She closed her eyes at the contact, and gave a barely-perceptible nod of her head. I wasn't sure what the nod meant, or if I'd just imagined it, but I decided that it meant she wanted me to kiss her again. So I did.

"Gabi, I need to tell you something," I said, running my fingers along her scalp as she rested her head against my chest.

"What is it?" I cringed at the worry in her voice, wondering what she thought I was about to say.

I tipped her head back so that I could look her in the eyes. "I'm sorry about the way I reacted this morning. I get why you felt like you needed to keep it a secret, and I know that it wasn't even about me. It was about protecting yourself, and I can respect that. But, I want you to know that you don't *have* to keep things from me, ok?"

She nodded her head, looking back at me with drooping eyes. "I accept your apology, and I forgive you. I understand why you reacted like you did, Terrence, you felt like you had been lied to. It hurts, I know, and I'm sorry that I made you feel like that. Do you forgive me?" She stifled a yawn as she finished speaking, then rested her head on my arm.

"Only if you let me carry you to your room so you can get some rest, and get you something cold to put on your face. It looks painful."

"It looks worse than it feels," she said, raising her hand to gingerly touch her cheek.

"I want to kick his ass even more now that I've seen your face. Tarryn is probably the only reason I'm not in jail right now. What happened after he hit you like that?"

"Well, the manager took me back in her office to call the police, but I talked her out of it. She got a cab for me, and I just came home. I have no idea where my parents or Michael went, but I hope it's back to Chicago. When they realized that I disappeared from the house, they caught a flight the next day. They planned on dragging me back home, and my dad got really upset when I told him I was never moving away from Atlanta."

We both looked up as a knock sounded at the door. Despite her tough front, Gabi was shaking. I walked up to the door, and glanced through the peephole into the hall. I couldn't keep my face from screwing up in annoyance as I turned to tell Gabi that it was her parents, with Michael in tow.

There was another knock, more powerful this time. It was the kind of knock that police use when they come to your door, and I could tell that it was meant for intimidation. These people were really starting to piss me off.

"They just won't give it a rest," Gabi whispered as fresh tears sprang to her eyes.

"Do you want to just ignore them?"

"No. I guess I just haven't been making myself clear enough or something, but they just keep pushing and pushing. It's tiresome, and... it's toxic. *They're* toxic."

"So what do you want to do?"

She slipped her hand into mine. "Open the door."

----*Gabi*----

"WHAT THE *HELL* is your problem, little girl?" My mother's voice, loud and dramatic as always, was the first thing to come through the door. It was shortly followed by it's owner, then my father, and then Michael, all of whom seemed shocked to see Terrence standing there, his fingers locked with mine.

I would have to thank him later, for looking so dangerously sexy as he stared down the three biggest stress factors in my life.

"I don't have one anymore, Mother." I turned to her, finally answering her question. "I just had a little epiphany, and as of tonight, none of you exist to me anymore. Problem solved."

"Are you telling me you're choosing this... *lawyer* over the life I've set up for you as a doctor's wife?" My father stepped forward with his fists clenched, but Terrence was right there. He released my hand so that he could cross his arms over his chest and then looked my father straight in the eyes, daring him to try to touch me again.

"I'm not choosing him, I'm choosing *me*. I am sick and tired of going back and forth with you guys about this. Until you can respect the fact that I am actually *not* a little girl, but a grown, capable woman who can make her own decisions, *you don't exist to me anymore*. And I mean that. If I have to get restraining orders, change phone numbers, emails, hire a bodyguard, whatever it takes, I will not let you harass me. I will not live by your rules. And... I won't end up being a punching bag, for either of you." I looked from my father to Michael, who at least had enough shame to avert his eyes. "I'm just done with the whole situation."

"So after everything we've done for you, this is how you show gratitude? Telling us we can't be in your life?"

I rolled my eyes. They always wanted to throw it in my face that they had given me a good life, as if it had actually taken them any extra effort. They had outsourced my parenting and love for my entire life, but the only thing they could *ever* say that they had given me was money. "You don't want gratitude, Dad. You want me to grovel and take orders. That's not going to happen. I do appreciate your investment into my future, even though I had to beg you to let me choose my own career. It would be stupid of me to offer to pay back my education, but I'll write you a check for every dime of the money you gave me when I moved. I don't need it. I have a job."

My father's mouth twisted into an ugly smirk, turning his handsome face into a mask that actually reflected the man he was. "You *think* you have a job. Did you forget that you work for my little brother? Neither of you will have a position at that firm by the time I get back to the car. You'll both be out on your asses, and I'll bet you'll be ready to come back home then."

"You do what you feel like you need to do," Terrence said, speaking for the first time as he reached for my hand. "Gabi and I will both be perfectly fine. If Mr. Graham does decide to fire us, that will just be what happens, but I don't give a shit about your threats. I'm not impressed, and neither is Gabi. I think it's time for you all to go."

"What are you, her bodyguard?"

"If I need to be." He squeezed my hand. "Please don't make me tell you again Mr. Jacobs. It's time to go." He took the few steps to the door and opened it wide, as if we were airing the apartment out.

"Gabrielle..." My father's voice was dangerously low as he stepped toward me, taking advantage of the fact that Terrence had momentarily left my side. "If we walk out of here today, we're done. No trust, no inheritance, no monthly allowance. *Nothing*. You're completely on your own, since you don't want to respect our wishes. Are you sure that's what you want?"

"I'm positive. Goodbye." I stood up a little straighter, bolstered by the finality of my words. It hit me right in the chest that I didn't even feel anything for the people I called Mom and Dad as they walked out of the door, not looking back.

I stopped Michael as he followed them. "This is the very last time I'm going to tell you that it's over between us. Do not call, write, text, nothing. If I see you anywhere near me again, I'm going to pursue legal action against you Michael, and it won't be pretty. And I'm not just talking about the police. I will wrap you up in so many civil lawsuits that getting insurance to open your own practice will be a fantasy. Goodbye."

He looked at me for a long moment, as if he were digesting my words for the first time. Then, he gave a slight nod to me, then Terrence, and practically bolted out of the door. When he was gone, Terrence closed and locked the door behind him, then immediately opened his arms for me.

I had to stop myself from running into them, but the instant he wrapped his arms around me, all of the tension and fear from just a few moments before melted away.

"Thank you for protecting me, and rescuing me. As always," I said, rising up on the tips of my toes for a kiss, which he obliged.

"You didn't need rescuing, Gabi. You were handling yourself fine, I was just making sure everybody kept their hands to themselves." He cupped my face, then leaned to kiss me again. "I'm proud of you, for standing up for yourself like that. You made a choice to live for *you*, and that's admirable."

I blushed, shaking my head. "You make it sound so profound, when really they were just getting on my damn nerves! I want the people that I love to be happy, but it can't be at the expense of my own health and sanity. I won't let anybody take that from me, not even my parents. They made their own choices, they have to deal with that. I'm not gonna lose any sleep about it."

I really wouldn't. I was honestly surprised that instead of feeling any sadness or remorse, I just felt *free*.

"I like this no-nonsense side of you," Terrence said, nuzzling his face into my neck. "This is sexy as hell."

"Oh, whatever." I smacked him playfully on the arm as I stifled another yawn. Terrence cupped my butt, lifting me so that I could wrap my legs around his waist as he carried me into my room. "Wait a minute, take me back to the kitchen, I'm hungry."

He laughed, but took me back into the kitchen, where he sat me down on the counter, but maintained his position between my legs. I leaned up for him to kiss me as I slid my fingers under his shirt, running them over the hard ripples of his abs.

"I thought you were hungry," he mumbled against my neck, the gently nipped at my ear.

"I can be hungry and horny at the same time. Are you complaining?"

"Absolutely not." He straightened his posture, staring at me as I snaked my fingers through his.

"What are you thinking about?"

He lifted one of my hands, pressing a kiss into my open palm. "I'm thinking about how much I love you, Gabi."

It took me a moment to register that he'd just declared his love for me. I waited for panic to set in, but it never came. Just an overwhelming sense of joy, and something that I hadn't felt for a long time before I met Terrence. *Peace.* There was no anxiety, no concern about if I was smart enough, pretty enough, and a whole long list of other 'enoughs' that I felt constant pressure about when I was with Michael. There was just peace. I wasn't so naive that I thought the perfection of this moment would be a constant, but I couldn't dwell on that. We would cross that bridge when we came to it.

I threw my arms around his neck, and kissed him with every bit of passion and energy I had left after the emotional events of the day. When we finally surfaced from the kiss, breathless, I had absolutely no fear when I leaned to tell him:

"I love you too."

GABI

I couldn't get my hands to stop shaking. Actually, I think *all* of me was shaking as I sat in Uncle Bobby's office, waiting. On what, I had no idea. Terrence and I had been stopped at the front desk by Vanessa, then herded into separate rooms. I had been sent to wait in Uncle Bobby's office, while Terrence had been directed into one of the smaller conference rooms.

It was the Monday after Christmas, just five days since the major blow up with my parents. I was still at peace with my decision to cut them out of my life, but the thought of Terrence losing his position at the firm because of me was making me nauseous.

When the door opened, I straightened my posture and did my best to keep my expression neutral. Uncle Bobby sat down across from me, with the usual hint of a smile playing on his face.

"Loosen up, Gabi-girl, you're not getting fired." He chuckled at the quiet, but excited shriek that I let out before jumping up to hug him around the neck. "Sit down, sweetheart, let me talk to you."

Still bubbling with excitement, I took my seat and tried to focus as he told me some rather interesting new information about my family.

Uncle Bobby met my mother first. For him, it had been love, immediately. For her, it had been a ticket to a wealthy life, on the arm of a handsome young lawyer. But as soon as she met my father, Bobby's older half-brother, she saw a bigger meal ticket. My father's medical practice was already well established in Chicago. He'd had a ten year head start on building the type of wealth that my mother was attracted to, so she'd dropped Bobby and moved on. They got married, and *very* shortly after, they had me.

"Gabrielle, there was a time that I thought you may have actually been my child, but the timing didn't add up. Even then, I still held out a secret little hope for a long time, especially once you started spending summers with your Aunt Pamela and I."

I was floored. Gold digging, sleeping with brothers, and secret love children? I would have never expected that type of scandal from my parents, but it actually explained a *lot*. Neither of them were ever particularly thrilled about summers I spent with my aunt and uncle. I could never understand why they would let me go *anyway*, when they didn't even seem to like them! Now, it occurred to me that they were afraid their secret might get leaked, so allowing them to have summers with me was a way of keeping my aunt and uncle quiet.

"Uncle Bobby... I called you, after my parents initially refused to allow me to go into law. Two days after I talked to you, I was in LSAT prep classes. Did you have something to with that?"

"I absolutely did. You called me in tears, and I wasn't going to sit back and allow them to crush your dream. So yes,

I played my card. I've played that card often over the years, sweetheart."

Uncle Bobby had started contacting me more and more when he found out I was pre-law, offering guidance on what classes to take, good study habits, tips on taking the bar, and upon graduation, one of the coveted junior associate positions at his firm. Even though my grades and test scores were excellent, I knew that I was only hired because of the letter of recommendation he'd written for me, and then presented to his fellow partners. Now, I *also* knew that he wasn't just doing me a favor. Helping me become a lawyer was his way of getting back at my parents!

My parents were *livid* when they found out I'd called my Uncle Bobby for a job. They claimed that the distance was the reason they didn't want me moving to Atlanta, but that was another half-truth. They were afraid that if I spent too much time with Uncle Bobby as an adult, we would end having this exact conversation.

"Wow. This is... this a lot. Um... I'm glad that you told me this, but I guess I'm just wondering why now?" I asked, relaxing back into the soft leather chair.

"Well, I received a call from your parents the day after Christmas, saying that you had denounced the entire family. Your father was demanding that I fire you and Mr. Whitaker." He stopped for a moment to chuckle. "I told your father that I hire and fire who I please, and that as long as your personal matters aren't affecting the quality of your work, they weren't relevant to your position here. I didn't hire you because you're my niece, I hired you because you're a bright young lawyer with incredible potential. Why on earth would I fire you on the whims of your parents, who I only tolerated *because of you*?"

"And Terrence? He told me that you warned him to stay away from me, is that true?"

"It absolutely is," he said, resting his elbows on his desk. "But, I would have given him that same warning about any beautiful young woman, it wasn't specific to you. Obviously, that warning has been ignored, but again, as long as your work isn't affected, I don't have a problem with it. I couldn't wish for a better suitor for you than Mr. Whitaker."

I sighed heavily, relief flooding through me as I realized we were going to be ok. Neither of us had spoken aloud about what we would do if we actually did lose our jobs, but it had certainly been on my mind, and I knew it was on Terrence's. We rode to the office together, in a heavy fog of silent worry that hadn't been completely lifted until now.

"Uncle Bobby, thank you so much. I'm sorry that I ended up causing drama."

"You didn't cause anything, sweetheart, your parents did. Your father made sure to let me know several times that he wasn't giving you a dime. I know you get a reasonable salary here, so you can cover your own expenses, but if you need *anything*, you don't hesitate to let me know, ok?"

"I won't." I walked around the desk to hug him again, and press a kiss into his cheek. "I'm gonna go get to work now, so you don't regret not firing me."

Uncle Bobby laughed, then stroked his chin. "Ah, about that... I don't think you and Mr. Whitaker are going to get any work done today. While you were waiting for me, the other partners and I welcomed him into the partner training program. He won't be starting officially until after he finishes his year with you, but I'm sure he'll want to celebrate. You kids go have fun."

I stopped at the door just before I left, turning to him to speak. "You and Vanessa... are you guys a 'thing'?"

"How do you know about that?"

"Uh... just a hunch," I lied, trying my best not to laugh at the surprised look on his face.

"Oh, well. Yes, we're a thing. We've been seeing each other for a few months now."

"Good for you, Uncle Bobby. She's a really sweet lady, and she's beautiful."

I said my goodbyes to him and then headed out, closing the door behind me. I could barely contain my excitement as I hurried down the hall to Terrence's office. As soon as I walked in, he locked the door behind me, and then swept me up into a hug.

"Congratulations baby," I told him, holding on to his arms as he placed me back on my feet.

"You knew, didn't you?" His eyes were sparkling with happiness as he gazed down at me. "That's part of the reason you couldn't tell me about Mr. Graham being your uncle. It would have messed up their plan."

He smiled as I nodded, then rested my head against his chest. "I wanted to tell you so badly that you really hadn't made a mistake, and that you weren't in trouble, but Uncle Bobby made me promise not to. It's also part of why I didn't want to complicate things between us. I couldn't be sure that my Uncle Bobby wouldn't find out and fire you over me. "

"Thank you for taking care of me, Gabi."

"You are very welcome, Mr. Whitaker."

"Mr. Whitaker?"

"Yes, we're at work. When we're here, everything has to be strictly professional. No touchy-feely stuff, ok?"

He cupped my butt, pulling me closer to his body. "You mean like that?"

"Yes, exactly like that."

"And what about this?" He placed a kiss on the bare flesh of my neck, then sucked the soft skin between his teeth, which we both knew would leave a mark.

"Exactly like that, stop it," I said, pushing him away as I laughed.

He came closer again, pulling me into his arms and pressing a kiss into the top of my head. "I love you, Ms. Jacobs."

Damn, I don't think I could ever get tired of hearing him say that. There wasn't a shred of doubt in mind that he meant it, every single time.

I raised my hand to do one of my favorite things, running my fingers through his beard. "I love you too, Mr. Whitaker."

2 Months Later

No fucking way.

"Gabi, where've you been, babe?" I smiled as Terrence pulled me closer to him on the bed, nuzzling his head into the back of my shoulder.

"I was just in the bathroom."

Just? Humph.

"It seemed like you were in there a long time."

I turned to face him, then starting tracing his eyebrows with my fingers. "Are you monitoring my bathroom time now?"

"No, the bed was cold when you left, I missed you."

Tell him now.

"You're such a baby about a cold bed." I playfully poked his shoulder, which he responded to by threatening to tickle me, which I hated.

"You already have me sleeping on these pink ass sheets when I stay with you, the least you could do is keep the bed warm," he complained, pretending to pout.

I wrapped my arms around his neck. "Aww, come here baby. I *know* how to keep you warm." I snaked my legs through his, moving closer so that our nude bodies were touching.

"Mmm, I like the sound of this. Are we going to need protection for what you have in mind?"

Tell him!

"No, actually." I released my arms from his neck and flopped back against my pillow. I let out a slow stream of breath as he sat up, propping himself on his elbow.

"Gabi, what's wrong?" He ran a hand along the side of my face, down my neck, between my breasts, and rested on my stomach. I covered his hand with my own and let out another stream of breath.

"You remember how we were really excited that first night we were together, on Christmas?"

"Yeah."

"How we had sex like four times, and didn't use any protection?"

"....Yeah."

"Well..." I reached over to grab the plastic baggie I had placed on the night stand on the way out of the bathroom. I placed it in his hand, watching to gauge his reaction as he recognized what it was.

"Huh. I guess that letter wasn't the only Christmas gift I gave you that night, was it?"

---the end... for now---

Did you enjoy this book? Please consider leaving me a review!
Want updates on new releases and Giveaways? Join my mailing list!
You can visit with me at www.beingmrsjones.com or https://www.
facebook.com/Christinacjones
I'm also on twitter, at @beingmrsjones

ABOUT THE AUTHOR

Christina C. Jones is a modern romance novelist who has penned many love stories. She has earned a reputation as a storyteller who seamlessly weaves the complexities of modern life into captivating tales of black romance.

ALSO BY CHRISTINA C JONES

Made in United States
North Haven, CT
17 May 2024

52594717R00114